Recompense

Recompense

Return to Oberammergau
Arnie P. Zimbelman

RECOMPENSE
RETURN TO OBERAMMERGAU

iUniverse books may be ordered through booksellers or by contacting:

iUniverse
1663 Liberty Drive
Bloomington, IN 47403
www.iuniverse.com
1-800-Authors (1-800-288-4677)

ISBN: 978-0-5951-2440-4 (sc)
ISBN: 978-1-4697-7137-3 (e)

Print information available on the last page.

iUniverse rev. date: 05/07/2015

To Iris
"I'll love you until the rivers run still,
and the four winds have all blown away."

EPIGRAPH

Seek
The Truth
~Constantly,
Diligently~But
Never Be Satisfied
That You Have Found It.
AZ

ACKNOWLEDGEMENTS

Special thanks go to my daughters, Deborah Hirsch, Terrie St. Clair, and Sherrie Zimbelman, for their interest, encouragement, and constructive comments as this work progressed; and to my son-in-law, Theo Omtzigt, for his computer wizardry.

Captain Shirley Autry, a pilot with United Airlines, provided invaluable advice and professional expertise through her review and suggestions regarding the near air disaster in the story.

Most of all, however, I owe a limitless debt of gratitude to my wife, Iris, who served as my computer typist, perceptive editor, gentle critic, and unending cheerleader. Without her, this novel would still be only an unrealized reverie in my mind.

CONTENTS

CHAPTER I

Brandon sat straight up in bed, startled and only partially awake, wondering what had roused him from his deep sleep. He looked at his alarm clock and saw that it was 6:10 a.m., twenty minutes before his usual wake-up time. What had he heard?

It came again: a firm, insistent knocking on the door of his apartment. Who could need him at this hour? He wasn't expecting any messages or deliveries, certainly nothing that required waking him so early.

Grabbing his robe, Brandon padded to the door and peered through the peep-hole. In the hall he saw a uniformed California Highway Patrol officer, sober-faced, erect, reaching to knock on the door once again.

Brandon relaxed. Oh, of course, he thought, this has to be about that case I've been working on, the toxic spill on 101 South. He unlocked the door and greeted the waiting patrolman, "Good morning, Officer. Is there something I can do for you?"

"Are you Brandon St.Clair?"

"Yes, I am. Is there some kind of problem?"

"Could I come inside for a few minutes, please? I have some important information for you, and I'd rather not talk out here."

"Sure, come on in. Here, sit down." Brandon was still not totally alert, but a vague sense of uneasiness was beginning to intrude, telling him that something more critical than environmental pollution was involved. "Could I fix you a cup of coffee?"

Recompense

"No, thank you, I won't be long. But I'm afraid the news isn't good." The patrolman cleared his throat. "Your parents have been traveling somewhere on the Mendocino coast, haven't they?"

Brandon's sense of foreboding deepened, and he sat down slowly opposite the patrolman. "Yes, they're spending the week-end up at Timber Cove Inn. Why, is something wrong?" Despite his best efforts, he felt panic rising in his chest.

"Well, Mr. St.Clair, I'm afraid there's been an accident…."

"An accident?" Brandon broke in. "Where? Are my parents all right? Were they hurt?"

"I'm sorry, but it was more serious than that." Again he paused, wiping his hand across his forehead. "You know how narrow Highway 1 is along that stretch of the coast, with all those hairpin curves. Well, it looks like when they were coming back down this way, their car was forced off the road."

"Oh my God, not along *that* road, right above the ocean! What happened? They're okay, aren't they?" By now Brandon's premonition of disaster was overpowering, bringing a chill to his entire being.

"I wish I knew a better way to tell you this, Mr. St.Clair, but the place where their car went over the edge is one of those where there's nothing below but rocks and Pacific Ocean." The patrolman's eyes reflected the pain of what he had to tell, as he added softly, "They never had a chance."

Brandon's eyes widened, shock and dread gripping him as the reality of the officer's words penetrated his consciousness. "You mean….don't tell me they're…." he halted, unable to articulate his fears.

"Yes, I'm afraid they're both dead. It looks like they died instantly, on impact. We didn't find the car until this morning, when a jogger spotted it down below and alerted us." The officer rose and put on his cap. "I'm very sorry to have to bring you this news, Mr. St.Clair. It's the hardest part of my job. I'm really very sorry."

Brandon remained seated, dazed and mute, trying to comprehend the terrible implications of what he had just been told. Was it possible? Could both his mother and father really be gone~just like that, with such brutal finality?

"I'd better be on my way now." The patrolman looked closely at Brandon. "Are you sure you'll be all right?"

Brandon nodded, still confused and unbelieving. He got to his feet, unsteadily, and followed the officer to the door. "You said they were forced off the road. Do you know what happened? What about the other car?" His training as a lawyer was beginning to come through.

"We're still not sure," the patrolman told him. "There were skid marks on the pavement, and we found some black paint scrapes on your parents' car. The other car must have come around that curve at a very high rate of speed and hit them. It was apparently a glancing collision, because the other car didn't stop. We're still investigating."

Brandon remained numb. At last he said quietly, "Is there anything else you can tell me, Officer?"

"All I can say is that I'm truly sorry, Mr. St. Clair. We'll keep you informed if anything new comes up. Meanwhile, we'll need you to come down and make positive identification, as soon as you're able." With that, he was gone.

For several moments, Brandon stood frozen, leaning against the closed door. Finally, mechanically, he made his way to the tidy apartment kitchen. He opened one of the cabinets and took down his coffee grinder and a bag of coffee beans.

Without warning, he felt a flash of pain so intense it seemed his skull would split, as a blinding, excruciating spasm of agony seared through his head.

*   *   *

Recompense

> ∞

"Your attention, please. Flight 1756 from San Francisco to Boston is now boarding at Gate 36."

Brandon looked at his watch, hesitated briefly, then decided he could delay a few more minutes since he had already picked up his boarding pass. He needed time to take a couple of aspirin. The beginnings of what he knew would be another vicious headache were just now crowding into the area of his left temple. Although experience told him the medication wouldn't really help much against the pain, he always felt a bit better for at least having tried.

He made his way quickly to a nearby fountain and gulped down the two tablets. I wonder what triggered it this time, he thought, as he hurried back to claim his spot in the boarding line. Having to deal with this type of agonizing discomfort was a relatively new experience.

He wasn't certain exactly how or why the headaches had begun. All he knew was that they came on unexpectedly, with no particular warning. The pattern was painfully familiar by now: a surge of intense pressure in his temple which became increasingly severe, recurring in a regular pattern of waves, each one more acute, until his head literally felt ready to explode. Then the throbbing would gradually subside, giving him a respite that sometimes lasted minutes, sometimes hours, before a new wave of pain developed. The pattern usually persisted for days.

But by now Brandon had also devised his own special means of coping with these debilitating episodes. It was quite simple, really, and usually at least partially effective. As the headache reached its torturous apex, he found that he could force his mind to drift into a state of what was almost semi-consciousness. By concentrating deeply on some other time, some other place, he learned that he could temporarily remove himself from the reality of the pain~actually, from *all* reality. This semi-hypnotic state did not erase the actual agony, but it did help to dull it somewhat. Additionally, it permitted his sense of imagination and fantasy to run free.

Now, as he moved slowly toward the smiling Attendant checking boarding passes, he could feel himself beginning to drift. Gradually, his mind began to convey him off toward the Sierras, to the magical blue of Lake Tahoe….

"Good morning, sir. Thank you for choosing United."

Automatically, he grinned as the Attendant's cheery greeting invaded his dream world. "Oh, good morning. Uh, nice day, isn't it?"

He made his way down the long ramp toward the waiting 747. Locating his assigned seat, he struggled to cram his carry-on bag into the small space remaining in the overhead bin. Then he pushed carefully past the two passengers seated between the aisle and his window seat and settled in.

Brandon had always been comfortable with flying, not hampered by the limited space allotted to coach-class passengers despite his six-foot frame. He tended toward a slight build, a feature his mother had often but unsuccessfully tried to remedy with her excellent home cooking. He smiled now as he thought of her, though the memory also brought renewed pangs of loss. How could he ever forget those gentle reminders?

"I wish you'd eat more, Brandon, I worry about you. I'm afraid you're too thin."

"It's okay, Mom, I've had more than enough. It was a great dinner, though, like all of yours. Thanks so much for asking me over."

"You're sure you couldn't have just a little more?"

"No thanks, Mom, really, I'm just fine." Then he'd add, with a twinkle in his eyes, "But I do appreciate your concern, even if I am twenty-eight years old. You and Dad have always been the very best!"

Their relationship had been open and affectionate, so a round of hugs was in order at any time, after which Brandon might hint, "You know, Mom, I probably wouldn't refuse one of those special desserts I saw out in the kitchen."

Recompense

∽

Inevitably, the conversation would shift at some point to his mother's most *basic* worry: "Brandon, you know how much Dad and I love you. But we won't always be able to be here like this. What we really hope is that you'll find a wonderful wife, someone for you to love, who'll love you in return." At that she would smile devotedly at her son. "And of course if she's a good cook, too, that will be a nice bonus."

Brandon remembered how he always greeted this suggestion with a chuckle, as he enveloped his petite mother in his arms. "Maybe someday, Mom, but not until I find someone as great as you are, someone who'll treat me exactly the way you treat Dad. I want my sweetheart to be my best friend for life, just like the two of you have always been. I really mean that. But right now, I have to concentrate on learning to be an effective lawyer, and doing well for the firm. You understand, don't you?" And so he'd put off her worries to another day.

He had loved his parents deeply. In fact, he had long been told that he was an absolute amalgam of the two. His temperament was much like that of his mother: loyal, sympathetic, organized perhaps to a fault, unyielding in matters of principle actually to the point of stubbornness. This last characteristic his father ascribed jokingly to her German heritage. By the same token, Brandon had fallen heir to his father's physical features: a full head of dark, slightly unruly hair, sensitive blue eyes, regular facial features just short of being handsome, culminating in the tiny cleft in his chin. His ready smile also seemed to have a shared ancestral origin, though he carried on the tradition as his own.

Finally free to allow his mind to slip into its reverie, Brandon closed his eyes, feeling his body relax despite the continuing pain of the headache. Mentally he began to shut out his surroundings, concentrating instead on visions of what lay ahead on this journey.

He was headed for Germany, using an air ticket that his mother and father had purchased some time ago. His parents had apparently planned a visit to Europe but wanted to see some old friends in Boston on their way, and so had arranged a cross-country flight with a layover there before continuing on. Brandon would instead connect with a flight going directly to Frankfurt, where he would join a pre-arranged tour taking its members to experience the decennial presentation of the Passion Play at Oberammergau. Not knowing exactly what to expect served to enhance his sense of anticipation.

Brandon began a dreamy visualization of the German countryside, which he really knew only from some travel magazines and a video he had rented. Its clean, precise beauty appealed to his sense of order and organization. And he was particularly pleased that it reflected care and concern for the natural environment, a characteristic especially close to his own most basic beliefs.

A sudden feeling of uneasiness broke the tranquility of these idyllic thoughts. He sat up straight, completely awake, eyes wide open, and looked around. What was it that had alerted him? Passengers were still boarding. Attendants were still doing their best to be helpful. But something significant had occurred, he was sure, except that he couldn't determine what it was.

He continued to scan the interior of the plane. His inspection halted unexpectedly when he spotted a woman several rows ahead, standing in the aisle, also staring quizzically at him. She was middle-aged, somewhat matronly in appearance, with silvery-gray hair and a kind, open, friendly face. She was wearing a white knit sweater over her print dress, and was holding a bulky cloth bag. Her entire appearance seemed to say, "Here's someone you can trust, someone you'd like to know."

What struck Brandon most forcefully, however, was the feeling that he *already* knew her. But how? From where? He had absolutely no idea. It was completely puzzling. And from the mystified look in the woman's eyes, she appeared to be thinking much the same thing about him.

The woman turned slowly toward her seat. With one last perplexed glance back at Brandon, she sat down out of his line of vision. But his mind continued to search, seeking some way to make the connection. He knew she was not associated with his circle of friends or acquaintances, nor was she a long-forgotten relative. Yet try as he might, he could not escape the feeling that *somewhere* they had met.

A resurgence of headache pain brought Brandon abruptly back to the present. The intense, penetrating bursts forced him once again to lie back in his seat, eyes closed, and attempt to return to his world of reverie.

This time, however, his thoughts did not take him immediately back to visions of Germany. Instead, he began to review in his mind the extraordinary set of circumstances that had brought him to be on this trip in the first place, going to a village that, as far as he knew, had no connection to his life whatsoever. Oberammergau? He didn't remember ever even having heard of the place until he found those tickets. Yet once he'd begun looking at the brochures, he'd felt a mystical, compelling urge to go.

His mind jumped back to the tickets. He had found them as he was going through his parents' things after the funeral. That thought took him back even farther to the events surrounding his parents' death. Had it been only six weeks ago? At times it seemed like it had been forever, then again like just yesterday. Tears welled in his eyes beneath the closed lids as he relived those awful moments when the Highway Patrolman had told him what had happened, that in an instant, his mother and father were gone.

For one thing he was grateful: the officer had remembered his promise to keep Brandon informed, and so had called during the past week to report that the hit-and-run driver had finally been located and apprehended farther up the coast, in Oregon. The arrest did not constitute a particular source of pleasure, but it did at least provide a small measure of closure.

Brandon and his parents had never been as close as some families were in the sense that they were all "pals". His parents had been older

when he was born, and as an only child they had given him every attention, but they had also maintained their own personal interests.
Extremely devoted to each other, they had still succeeded in making
Brandon feel totally loved and secure. As a result, he had developed a
respect for them that bordered on awe. Above all, he did not want to
disappoint them, a factor at least partially responsible for his success as
a budding trial lawyer. Still, his sense of loss was overwhelming. Soon
after the accident, the headaches had begun.

Brandon remembered the funeral only vaguely. It had seemed almost
surreal, with him as a detached observer more than a grieving son. In their
usual thoughtful and meticulous manner, his parents had pre-arranged all
of the details for both their funeral services and their burials years earlier,
so that all he had to do was set everything in motion. Without those
arrangements, he wasn't sure he could have survived the ordeal. As events
unfolded, he could only think appreciatively: This is so typical of what I've
learned to expect from you, Mom and Dad.

It was after all of this had passed, when friends and distant relatives
were gone and he was alone once more that the finality of the void had
begun to register. What should he do? His mother and father had always
just *been* there, and now there was no one.

While he considered his next steps, Brandon had asked for time off at
his law firm. He had just finished a difficult case, one in which he had suc-
cessfully defended a young woman accused of murdering her husband.
He had convinced the jury that the woman acted in self-defense: after
enduring six years of brutal domestic violence, she was justified, Brandon
argued, in shooting her husband with his own weapon when he threatened her once again. The fact that Brandon had taken the case *pro bono*
did not seem to matter to the firm as much as that justice was served, and
the conclusion seemed to be ample reward for everyone. Still, it had been
an exhausting period, especially so soon after the death of his parents,
and the senior partners agreed that Brandon had earned some time away.

Recompense

This was when he had decided to go through his parents' effects. He felt it might be therapeutic, help him to cope, while at the same time it would enable him to hold onto the pleasant memories of their time together for just a little longer.

All of the business arrangements were in order, as anticipated, so that he had been able to resolve the financial matters rather quickly. The small, charming Victorian dwelling which had been "home" until he moved to his own apartment contained so much of the spirit of his parents that he had not had the heart to sell it. Instead, he decided to give up his own apartment and move back to the familiar surroundings where he had known so much joy and security. This enabled him to progress slowly with the disposition of the personal effects his parents had left behind, and it was then that he had found the tickets.

They were tucked inside a packet marked "Travel" which he found in the small wall safe, along with brochures about their intended destination. Oh yes, Brandon had thought as he thumbed through the pamphlets, I remember Mom and Dad planning a trip to Europe, but I don't think they ever told me where they were actually going. Evidently they had decided on Oberammergau, where a Passion Play depicting the final week of the life of Christ was presented during the summer of every tenth year. Exactly why they had selected this event he wasn't sure. It may have been that, considering their ages, his parents concluded this could be their last opportunity to attend.

Reading the brochures inspired Brandon to do research on the Internet, where he found additional background on this unique event. He found that it had begun in 1634 as a result of the Black Plague, which was then ravaging Europe. This insidious contagion, carried by flea-infested rats, had swept across the continent in successive waves after being introduced from the Middle East through Italian ports. Its spread during the 1600's had been intensified by the depredations of the

Thirty Years' War as marauding armies, mercenaries, and deserters overran the countryside.

Consequences were horrifying, both socially and economically. With no concept as to the cause of the epidemic, the populace panicked. Some blamed demons, others a "miasma" in the air, but no one had a remedy. Huge fires were lighted at town entrances to burn away the evil vapors. In other areas inhabitants simply fled, thus helping to spread the pestilential syndrome. Few able-bodied citizens were left to tend the fields, which often left the general population too weak from lack of food to resist the affliction. Starvation added to the grim total. Before it burned itself out, the Black Plague was estimated to have taken the lives of between one-third and one-half of the inhabitants of Western Europe.

As early as 1632, in an effort to prevent anyone from bringing this deadly malady into their tiny Alpine village, the town fathers of Oberammergau had ordered armed guards posted at all town entrances to keep out any visitors. Unfortunately, this exclusion also affected residents of the hamlet who happened to be away at the time the ban was instituted.

According to popular accounts, this latter category included a young laborer named Kaspar Schisler, who had left his wife and children in Oberammergau for the summer to work in another village on the other side of the Alps. Homesick for his young family by summer's end, Schisler devised a means to slip past the guards and return to his home. What he didn't realize at the time~or if he did realize it, he did not let it deter him~was that he had already contracted the fatal disease. Shortly after the reunion with his family, Schisler was dead.

The family reported that he had died of natural causes. However, the truth soon became apparent when other members of his family also succumbed to what was obviously the plague. Efforts at isolation had failed.

Panic set in as the epidemic spread. Some residents locked themselves into their homes. Others wailed in the streets, or gathered to pray at the local church in hopes of a cure. The unfortunate result was that even *more* villagers were contaminated as the plague continued its virulent course. In the ensuing weeks, eighty-four residents~about one-tenth of the town's population~succumbed to the "Black Death."

Village officials, helpless to stem the fatal tide, attempted one last desperate measure: they made a vow. If God would spare the rest of the residents, they pledged, every ten years from then on~forever!~the town would present a play that would depict the suffering and death of Jesus Christ. Miraculously, according to local legend, the plague claimed no more lives in Oberammergau.

The grateful town held its first Passion Play in 1634, portraying the story of Christ's life from the time of His triumphal entry into Jerusalem through His trial, crucifixion, resurrection, and transfiguration. The initial performance was held in the parish church, and those who attended were largely residents of the village. But as the years passed and word of the Play spread, performances moved outdoors, first to the churchyard and ultimately to a facility designed and built specifically for Passion Play performances.

Productions continued each decade through 1674, when dates of the event were changed to coincide with the beginning of each new calendar decade, in this case, 1680. This practice was followed thereafter to the present time.

There were some aberrations. It appears that a crisis was precipitated in the 1770's when, by edict of Elector Maximilian Joseph, performance of any religious plays in Bavaria was forbidden. Oberammergau appealed the restriction, but accounts remain hazy as to whether any productions actually took place. In 1810, upheavals caused by the Napoleonic Wars postponed the drama for one year. Similarly, World War I forced delay of any performances from 1920 to 1922, and the Play scheduled for 1940 was never held, since many of the villagers had been drafted into the German army during the Nazi regime. The village itself was not adversely affected by World War II, so the Play resumed in 1950, at the behest of American occupation forces. Other variations occurred in 1934 and 1984, when special presentations of the Play were held to commemorate the 300th and 350th anniversaries of its origin in 1634.

Why he found all of this so fascinating Brandon wasn't sure. Originally, when he had discovered the tickets for the tour, he had planned to cash them in, since a receipt for trip cancellation insurance was among the items in the packet. However, the more he read, the more intrigued he became. It was as though a magnetic force was drawing him toward this mysterious place with which he felt a psychic bond. Ultimately, his curiosity won out. He *had* to go.

He made the decision to cash in only one ticket and use the other. This did not present a problem, since his father's first name had also been "Brandon," though he was known as "Brad" by most of his friends. So Brandon had been able to take advantage of all of the arrangements his father had made. It made the trip more affordable, and he hoped he might also discover why this destination had held such an attraction for his parents.

With the plane now safely on its way, he could feel the throbbing headache pain gradually begin to ease. He took several deep breaths, pressed his fingers briefly against his eyes, and then casually surveyed his fellow passengers. He had not seen the woman whose identity had so intrigued him since she had taken her seat. But suddenly she reappeared. With the "Fasten Seatbelt" sign turned off, she was making her way in his direction from her seat up ahead, perhaps toward the restrooms in the rear. Brandon again experienced an inexplicable sense of recognition as she approached, though he still could not determine why. What was going on, he wondered?

As the woman passed his row, she hesitated a moment, looking directly at him. She opened her mouth briefly as though to ask a question, then lowered her gaze and moved on. As she passed, Brandon sensed something even more mystifying: the unmistakable aroma of fresh-baked cookies wafting faintly through the air after her.

Unable to take his eyes from this enigmatic individual, he watched as she continued toward the rear of the plane. So it was that he observed a further baffling occurrence. At one of the seats a few rows behind Brandon, the woman halted again, peering intently at the man sitting next to the aisle. With the same questioning look she had fixed on Brandon earlier, she now studied this man. Apparently unable to resolve this second instance of seeming recognition, she nodded, smiled uncertainly, and moved on. Once again she glanced back, as she had done before, only this time her quizzical gaze took in both the new man and Brandon. With a puzzled shake of her head, the woman resumed her progress down the aisle.

The new man had been returning her visual scrutiny, but now he shifted his perplexed look toward Brandon. For a brief instant his eyes also widened in apparent remembrance, and he smiled. Then a look of consternation crossed his face, as though he was embarrassed by this obvious case of mistaken identity.

Still, as Brandon returned the smile, the man continued to stare. Like the woman, he was middle-aged, a short, solid individual who looked like he would perhaps be more at home in a steel mill than on a cross-country flight. He was dressed well enough in a rather out-dated sport coat and open-collared polo shirt. But there was an uneasiness about him that indicated travel was perhaps not his usual forte.

Brandon finally turned away, but with an even deeper sense of confusion. How could he explain what was happening? Who were these people? What was this hidden "connection" they seemed to have with him?

The journey ahead promised to be intriguing!

CHAPTER II

The touchdown at Boston International Airport was routine. As passengers slowly gathered their carry-on items to leave the plane, Brandon glanced once more at the two people who held such special interest for him.

The woman was looking back at him as well. Her friendly face broke into a warm smile, in spite of the continuing hint of bewilderment in her eyes. Taking her flight case and the cloth bag that appeared to contain knitting materials from the overhead bin, she joined the parade of travelers exiting past the personable Attendants and on up the ramp.

The man who had been seated behind Brandon was also in the process of collecting his belongings, but was having more difficulty. He struggled with his carry-on items, which included a large old-fashioned satchel, an overcoat, a plastic bag with food items protruding, plus several paperback books. Oblivious to frowns exchanged by his two fidgeting seatmates, he finally got a firm grip on all of the articles and began his bumbling exit.

When Brandon reached the waiting room, he moved off to a quiet area where he could consider his course of action. There would be a two-hour wait for his plane to Frankfurt~just enough time to retrieve his larger bag at the luggage carousel and catch the shuttle to the Lufthansa terminal.

This inconvenience, he knew, resulted from the plans his parents had made for their layover in Boston. Since he had rescheduled his connecting flight, Brandon would be taking a different airline for the rest of the trip, so now he would have to rush to be on time. He was always uncomfortable with hurried timetables and tight deadlines such as these. His customary method of operation was to plan well in advance, organize thoroughly, and then adhere strictly to his established routine.

The arrangements went smoothly enough, however, leaving Brandon extra time before the Lufthansa flight departed for Frankfurt. With his bag checked, he settled into one of the chairs in the waiting area. He had nothing to do now but relax and scrutinize the passengers who would soon be his new traveling companions.

Then he spotted her: the woman from the plane. She was seated in the same waiting area, with her knitting bag in her lap and her fingers swiftly crafting a small pink sweater from a ball of yarn. So far she hadn't noticed Brandon, but as he continued his observation, she suddenly looked up from her knitting and gazed directly at him. Again there was a momentary flicker of recognition, again a soft smile and a slight shake of her head.

As though drawn by some elusive force, Brandon found himself taking an action contrary to his usual systematic nature: slowly he got up and approached the woman, though she was a complete stranger. His movements brought a brief hint of anxiety to her eyes, replaced almost instantly by a look of welcome. It seemed that she, too, was eager to resolve the mystery of their mutual attraction.

Nearing the spot where the woman was seated, Brandon stopped still. There it was again: that distinct but vague scent of baking cookies. Where could it be coming from, he wondered, glancing around. Hesitantly, he sat down beside the waiting woman.

"Hello," he began, "my name is Brandon St. Clair." He paused, uncertain how to pose his question. "Why do I have this unexplainable feeling that we know each other?"

The woman greeted him warmly. "Nice to meet you, Brandon. My name is Louise Scheer, and I have to admit I had the same feeling when

I first saw you on the plane. But I can't seem to remember, either, where we might have met."

"Do you happen to be from San Francisco?"

"No, my hometown is Mendocino, a little way up the coast from there. Do you ever get up that way?"

"Oh sure, I used to go there often with my parents." As memories of those happy days flashed through his mind, Brandon once more felt the sharp pang of loss and aloneness. "They're gone now," he finished softly.

"Oh, I'm so sorry." Mrs. Scheer reflected sincere empathy in both her speech and her warm blue eyes.

Quickly Brandon continued, "Do you work in Mendocino? Could I have seen you in one of those quaint little shops up there?"

Mrs. Scheer's eyes lit as she sensed a possible solution to the mystery. "Of course, that must be it. I have a little Bake Shoppe on Front Street, not far from Headlands State Park. You can tell I always test all my products myself," she laughed, patting her stomach. "I'll bet you stopped in sometime for one of my special macadamia nut cookies."

"Sure, that's very possible. I'm famous for never passing up a chance to nab one of those. We must have come by your shop when we were up that way." Still, he didn't actually remember having met her, though it might explain the aroma he kept noticing.

Bringing his thoughts back to the present, Brandon asked, "Are you on flight 1756 too?"

"Yes, I am." Mrs. Scheer almost glowed as she continued, "When we get to Frankfurt, I'll be flying on to Munich."

"And then?"

"Oberammergau. The Passion Play, a long-time dream of mine. To go, I mean."

Brandon's eyes widened in surprise. "What a coincidence! That's where I'm headed, too."

Recompense

Mrs. Scheer looked pleased. "My, that really *is* a coincidence. Who knows, maybe we'll meet again there. Wouldn't that be nice?" She shook her head. "With the thousands of people who go to see the Play, though, I suppose that's not too likely."

"You're probably right," Brandon concurred. "Well, it's been very pleasant chatting with you. Good luck on the rest of your trip."

"Thank you, and the same to you."

Their exchange had been interrupted by the announcement: "Ladies and gentlemen, Lufthansa Flight 1756 to Frankfurt is now boarding at Gate 23. We are asking that all passengers with special seating requirements board at this time. Thank you for your patience."

Mrs. Scheer gathered her carry-on items and started for the boarding line forming for regular passengers. Brandon followed close behind. As they waited their turn, he renewed their conversation.

"Do you have relatives in Germany?"

"None that I know of. But I am of German ancestry. My family immigrated sometime in the early 1800's. So did my husband's. I understand they even changed their name to sound more American. It used to be pronounced Scheerer, but they dropped the last syllable."

"I guess that happened to lots of families~sometimes on purpose, sometimes by accident. Do you have a family of your own now?"

"No, there's just me. I lost my husband many years ago. I guess my Bake Shoppe and my customers are my family now." She became pensive for a moment. "I did always wish we'd had a daughter, though," she added wistfully. Then she brightened. "But this makes it easier for me to get away."

"It's about the same for me," Brandon said. He wasn't ready to relay the real circumstances that had brought him to this place at this time.

By now they had reached the boarding ramp. Moving steadily toward the waiting plane, they found little time for further pleasantries. Brandon was thankful that they were about ready for departure, since the memories of his parents had also brought back reminders of his bereavement. He could feel the pressure of headache pain begin to crowd into his temple once more.

Finding his assigned seat, Brandon stored his personal luggage overhead and settled back. He always enjoyed observing the actions of fellow travelers in situations like this, viewing their spontaneous responses as glimpses into their personalities. Some feigned a blasé or bored attitude, which he suspected was a possible cover-up for personal insecurities. Others demonstrated either the courteous, thoughtful demeanor or the rudeness that was perhaps the hallmark of their daily lives. It had long been Brandon's contention that one true measure of any person's character was how he or she treated "service" personnel.

Now his scrutiny brought unanticipated consequences, however. Among the approaching passengers was the man who had caught his attention on the previous flight. Here he was again, struggling down the aisle with his varied assortment of carry-on items, looking around uncertainly for his seat number. When he spotted Brandon, he stopped, and for an instant his eyes sparkled as though he had unexpectedly seen an old friend. A smile crossed his broad face. Then the look of puzzlement and confusion returned, and he shuffled on to the rear of the airplane.

Brandon was not prepared for what followed. As the next group of passengers moved toward him, he felt once again an overpowering surge of recognition, much like what he had experienced when he first saw Mrs. Scheer. But this time the feeling was magnified, multiplied. There were at least half a dozen individuals who, for whatever reason, appeared distinctly familiar! It was totally incomprehensible, yet it was undeniable.

The first man was a priest, Brandon could tell, from the clerical collar under his dark jacket, as well as by the cross suspended from a chain around his neck. He appeared to be about twenty years older than Brandon, almost as tall. Watching the ease of his movements, Brandon made an assessment: In this man, the Church gained a dedicated advocate, he thought, but I'll bet the world lost a good athlete.

Next came a family of four, with the smartly-dressed parents arguing and the two pudgy children complaining. The girl was a young teen, the boy several years her junior. While the youngsters' faces were not unattractive, they looked like they had been molded by a lifetime of perpetual pouting. The whine in their voices only furthered the impression that here were two "spoiled brats." Brandon couldn't help but hope they wouldn't be seated anywhere close by.

Lagging some distance behind the family, as though fearful somehow of being associated with them, was a tall, slender woman in a classically tailored tweed suit. Her plain but pleasant face, surrounded by short, straight black hair, capped her no-nonsense appearance. From a strap over her shoulder hung an expensive-looking camera, which she carefully protected. After placing her trench coat and small bag neatly in an overhead bin, she settled gracefully into her seat.

Totally taken aback, Brandon tried to sort out what was happening. Who *were* these individuals? Why did he have this peculiar feeling that he knew them *all*? Was it only the throbbing of his renewed headache that was confusing him, or did he actually have some connection with them, past or present?

Exhausted from the combination of surging pain in his temple and turmoil in his mind, Brandon closed his burning eyes and drifted off into another reverie.

CHAPTER III

In his state of semi-consciousness, Brandon was only marginally aware of last minute preparations for take-off, or of the smooth entry into the atmosphere by Lufthansa Flight 1756. He could hear solicitous Flight Attendants offering drinks and other refreshments, but his mind was too clouded to respond to what was occurring around him. He thought he remembered vaguely that on one occasion the pilot had come through the cabin, chatting with the passengers. But as the headache pain intensified, he retreated ever deeper into his private inner world.

So it was that he suddenly found himself far away, in a place he seemed to recognize and yet didn't really know. Was he dreaming, he wondered? Was this a vision, or a trance? Or was this a place he had actually been to long ago, since the impressions were so vivid? He was completely puzzled.

What he was experiencing was a small village, set in a mountain valley ringed by forest-covered mountains. One peak was particularly distinctive. It served almost as a back-drop for the village, hovering over it in a protective posture. The stance was not threatening, but rather one that gave stability and dignity to the town below. Over everything hung a hint of the surreal, like a scene shrouded in mist.

Looking around in wonder, Brandon discovered himself in a narrow winding street with Alpine buildings lining both sides. Some were homes, some shops, others a combination in which the family lived upstairs over their workplace on the ground floor. Bright red and pink flowers bloomed in profusion in boxes attached under windows and along balconies of many of the buildings. Others were adorned with elaborate, colorful murals. The atmosphere was quiet and peaceful, a truly pastoral setting.

But something was missing. For a few moments Brandon could only glance about, perplexed. Then he realized what was so strange: he was the only one there! No people, no activity, no sounds broke the silence, as though the village had been mysteriously abandoned. Hesitantly, he wandered down the little street, but to no avail. No matter how much he searched, Brandon knew he was alone.

Why would such an enchanting Alpine hamlet be deserted? There must be a reason, though he was unable to discover a single clue to the secret.

From far in the distance, Brandon seemed to hear someone calling: "I'm sorry, sir, but would you like…."

The voice faded away, then returned with renewed urgency: "Sir, would you like…."

Cautiously, Brandon opened his eyes. There he was, back on the familiar airliner. An attractive young Flight Attendant, with distinct remnants of her German accent, was repeating, "Sir, what would you like for your dinner? I hated to wake you," she added, "but I'm afraid I can't wait any longer to serve you."

Brandon blinked several times and looked around, still in the throes of his reverie. Had he been asleep? Was it really just a dream? Slowly gathering his thoughts, he straightened in his seat, smiled wanly at the Attendant, and responded, "I'm sorry, I must have dozed off. What was your question?"

The Attendant returned his smile. "I just wanted to know what you would like for dinner, sir, chicken or pasta." She hesitated a moment. "They're both quite good."

"I'll try the pasta, then. And thanks for waking me up."

"You're most welcome, sir. And to drink?"

"Coffee, please."

"Thank you. I'll be right back." She moved on down the aisle.

Brandon took a deep breath. He looked around at his fellow passengers and concluded that everything was quite normal. But where had he been? What was that secret village he had visited? He was sure it was not merely his imagination, since it had been so real. And yet, here he was, right where he had always been, on an airplane headed for Frankfurt. It didn't make sense.

Mentally adding one more incident to the series of unexplainable occurrences that had taken place since he began this trip, Brandon decided to shut everything out of his mind. If he couldn't figure it out, he would ignore it. After all, he could still anticipate many pleasant happenings ahead as his journey unfolded.

A movie was playing on the cabin screen, but Brandon wasn't interested. Having finished his dinner, he decided he would just enjoy the trip and try to get some sleep. The headache pain had left, at least temporarily, so he closed his eyes again, relaxed as best he could, and shut out all thoughts of his surroundings. Maybe he'd even be able to go back to that village….

The low hum of voices and quiet stirrings of fellow passengers intruded into Brandon's peaceful world. He straightened up, rubbed his eyes, and looked around. Morning light was beginning to fill the airplane cabin. Some travelers were still asleep in varied positions, while others talked quietly or moved about, going to and from the restrooms. Attendants were busily preparing to serve breakfast. Checking his watch, Brandon realized it would not be too long before they reached their destination.

Upon arrival at the Frankfurt terminal, passengers were greeted by the usual bustle. People held up signs to welcome friends, or to direct individual travelers and tour groups. Brandon looked around, trying to find his way to the luggage area. There he was to meet his tour manager for the first time, as well as the travelers with whom he would be spending the next twelve days.

The tour director, who introduced herself as Herta Steiner, was a cheerful, good-natured young woman who greeted each member of the group personally as they straggled in. As Brandon viewed the cluster of people gathering around her, however, he felt a sudden tense, constricting chill. This just can't be, he thought, it's too unbelievable! There, in the waiting group, was every one of the passengers he had seemed to recognize on the airplane! They were all going to be on the same tour! This included the friendly Mrs. Scheer, the man with the bulging satchel, the priest, the contentious family of four, and the tall, slim, methodical woman. Surely, coincidence was being stretched to absurdity!

A wave of misgiving swept over Brandon. What was going on here? He glanced around, dismayed by the ongoing series of bizarre developments. It was just too much!

Then, taking a few deep breaths, he began to relax and reassess the situation. What was there to be concerned about? Did anyone appear to be hostile or threatening? No. Instead, they all seemed downright neighborly, chatting amicably with one another.

Mrs. Scheer came over to where he was standing, exclaiming excitedly, "Brandon, would you have believed it? We're going to be travel partners after all!"

"You're right, Mrs. Scheer. It does seem rather incredible, doesn't it?"

The sole exception to the unity was the family of four, who stood off to one side, the children still complaining and the parents still bickering. Frankly, Brandon hoped they would continue to remain aloof.

Calling for attention in her accented voice, Herta Steiner welcomed the group warmly. Briefly, she described their upcoming itinerary: "We will all be transferring as a group for the short flight to Munich, where we will have an afternoon of sight-seeing. After two nights in Munich, we will continue on by motor coach to Salzburg, Austria, and to

Innsbruck. From there, the tour will take us along the Alpine Road for visits to two of Mad King Ludwig's exotic castles, and to several other stops in the Bavarian region of Germany. We'll end our tour in Oberammergau, where we'll view a performance of the Passion Play."

Herta beamed at the group. "I presume the Play is the main reason a lot of you chose this particular tour, am I right?" From the nods of agreement, Brandon surmised that Oberammergau was indeed the ultimate goal for most of his traveling companions.

In a mood of friendly camaraderie, the group was on its way. From now on, Herta told them, their luggage, plus all accommodations, would be handled by the tour company, leaving the travelers free to enjoy the sights they had come so far to see.

"We'll take care of the routine house-keeping chores, so you can relax as you see all that our beautiful region has to offer," Herta said with a smile. This, Brandon concluded, was his style of travel. He was only too happy to pay to have someone else do the things he found unpleasant.

Munich proved to be a perfect introduction to the wonders of Bavaria. Brandon had always been intrigued by diverse architectural styles, one of the reasons he'd chosen to remain in San Francisco. The afternoon city tour revealed a whole new world of architectural marvels, with only one negative feature: he found he sincerely appreciated everything in Munich except the stolid, unimaginative buildings constructed during the Nazi era. They seemed out of place in a city characterized by Gothic charm.

The Marianplatz, with its elaborate City Hall and tinkling Glockenspiel, was particularly intriguing to Brandon. He had a penchant for observing things from the highest possible vantage point, so now he made his way up the three-hundred steps of St. Peter's bell tower and looked down from above on the square below. As far as he was concerned, this view alone made the trip worthwhile.

Recompense

That evening, at the "Welcome" dinner at their hotel, Brandon began to learn more about the people with whom he would be spending the next days. He had found an empty chair next to Mrs. Scheer.

"Why, hello, Brandon," she greeted him. "It's so nice of you to join me."

Brandon smiled at her welcome. "What do you think of Munich so far?"

"Oh, it's just wonderful! I had no idea we'd be seeing anything quite so magnificent as the City Hall. I just loved those little Glockenspiel characters."

"Yes, so did I. And this is only our first stop. If Munich is any indication, I think we're in for a real treat."

The servers broke into their exchange, bringing a dinner designed to give the visitors an introduction to German cuisine. Following the salad came wienerschnitzel with a light wine sauce, spaetzle, and red cabbage, all delicately flavored. The complimentary Rhine wine was some of the best Brandon could remember having tasted, and the Black Forest cake for dessert provided the perfect finishing touch to their German meal.

Comments by the group were universally complimentary, except for the two youngsters. "We don't like this stuff," they fussed, "we don't even know what it is." They refused to try anything until the accommodating staff brought them hamburgers and French fries, at Herta's special request.

After dinner, introductions all around enabled Brandon to begin to associate faces of individuals with their names, provided on a roster. The tour group consisted of a total of twenty-nine people: the director, their bus driver Rudolph, and twenty-seven travelers.

So far the only names he had learned were those of Mrs. Scheer, Herta Steiner, and Rudolph. Now he found that the man he had first seen on the San Francisco-to-Boston flight was Herman Meyer, the priest was Father Hochburg, the family of four was the Grossfeldts, and the tall woman was Miss Margaret Wilson. Many of the remaining tour members indicated, either by their names or comments, that they too were of German ancestry. Mr. Grossfeldt let it be known that *his* reason for being there was that he had won this "all-expenses-paid" trip for four in a contest at work. Still, to most, the evening appeared strangely to take on the aura of a "homecoming."

Mellowed by the fine food and excellent wine, as well as the friendly conversation, Brandon could feel his apprehensions begin to melt away. "It's going to be a great trip," he told himself, "with exciting new vistas." So what if he couldn't explain some of the strange things that had been going on. Did that really matter?

Still, deep down, Brandon knew he was only deluding himself. By training and by natural inclination, he liked to believe every problem had a logical solution, that most things in life could be kept organized and in order. Yet much as he hated to admit it, events he had been encountering so far were well beyond his understanding, and a disturbing question kept crowding into his thoughts: How can I figure out what's going to happen *next*?

CHAPTER IV

A wake-up call from the hotel switchboard roused Brandon to a new day of adventure. This morning, Herta had told the group, they would tour Nymphenburg Palace with its elegant gardens, and then visit the Deutches Museum on the Isar River. After that, they would have the afternoon free to enjoy Munich on their own before reuniting for dinner at the Hofbrauhaus. It all sounded appealing. Brandon found he was adapting easily to the regimen of touring with a group. He didn't like having to make his own arrangements, so he appreciated the effort that had gone into making this journey so care-free for the tour members.

He was not disappointed. It was a leisurely day filled with new experiences, and he savored them all. Even the evening's entertainment at the Hofbrauhaus, with its raucous activities stimulated by huge steins of beer, proved to be an interesting interlude.

The evening also provided his first opportunity to become better acquainted with fellow tourist Herman Meyer. Having disposed of an enormous stein, Mr. Meyer overcame his customary reticence and took a seat across the table from Brandon.

"You're the one they call Brandon St. Clair, aren't you?" he began somewhat hesitantly.

"Yes, I am. And you're Mr. Meyer, right?"

"Ach no, no, not Mr. Meyer," he protested. "I'm chust plain Herman." He gave a short laugh. "But St. Clair doesn't sound German. Do you have people here in Germany?

Brandon took a sip from his stein. "I don't think so. I know that my mother's family came from somewhere in southern Germany many years ago. But no one I know has ever done a genealogical study."

"That's too bad," Herman mused. "Everyone should know about his family." He was silent for a moment, then added, "Maybe *you* should do it."

Brandon laughed. "I don't really think so. But I wouldn't mind someone else doing it for me."

"It's not so hard. You could start while you're here, snooping through some old church records. They always kept track of everybody."

"Hmmm! Could be interesting. But I'd rather not miss out on the regular agenda Herta has planned. Maybe that will give me an excuse to come back, though."

"Yah, that's goot, that's goot," Herman agreed.

"How about you, Herman? Do you have relatives still living over here?"

"Oh yah. I'm hoping to visit my uncle when we go through Garmisch-Partenkirchen. He lives close by there. I wrote him saying I'm coming." Herman grinned. "I even brought along presents for the young ones, in my satchel."

"Good for you. It must be nice having people who care about you this far away from home," Brandon said, somewhat wistfully.

Their conversation was interrupted as the Bavarian brass band returned from its break and once again filled the large hall with its "Oompah" tempo. Herman nodded, and left to rejoin those enthusiastically dancing the polkas. Still, Brandon had enjoyed the exchange with the likable little man, and hoped he might have found a new friend.

The next day was a "make-believe" day for Brandon. Following the short drive across the Austrian border to Salzburg, a city whose wealth, they were told, had been built on its salt mines, the group checked into their hotel in the older part of the city. When Brandon crossed to his window to check the view, he gave an involuntary gasp. There, directly before him, rose the Hohensalzburg Castle, its majestic, stalwart presence holding guard over the city below. It was a magnificent sight. And even better, Herta had promised they'd be visiting the castle after lunch.

The sight from the castle walls, with the city spread below, was more breath-taking than Brandon could have imagined. He noted Margaret Wilson moving about with her camera, busily recording the panorama from different angles. I'll bet she's a professional photographer, he guessed.

Louise Scheer joined him as he gazed down from the ramparts, voicing her opinion of the view in awed tones: "Isn't it just wonderful, Brandon? Can you believe it? It's like stepping back in history, into a whole different time period!"

"Absolutely! There's an Old World charm about this place we just can't match in our country."

"And I thought we couldn't possibly see a city prettier than Munich."

"Me too! It may sound like I'm betraying Munich, but I think I've just discovered a new 'favorite city'."

Adding to the charm was a small cemetery behind the castle, with delicately-wrought, intricate iron grave markers. But Herta pointed out an even more fascinating item lower down, below the castle hill.

"Can you all see that little stone house down there? Over there, in the middle of the green?"

The house was totally isolated, set apart completely by itself. "That was the home of the Executioner. Either he didn't want to live near anyone else, or they didn't want to live near him. My guess is it was the latter," she explained, with a laugh.

If the view from the castle was spectacular, the rest of the city was at least equal in enchantment for Brandon. Herta led the group for a quick visit to the Domplatz, containing the Archbishop's Residenz and the Cathedral, suggesting that they return later for a longer look on their own. They moved on past the old Horse Trough, with its equestrian statuary and frescoes, to Mozart's birthplace. For Brandon, who loved all types of classical music, but particularly that of Mozart, to be at the actual birthplace of such genius was overpowering.

Finally, Herta turned them loose on one of Old Salzburg's major shopping streets, Getreidsgasse, with the light-hearted admonition, "Be sure to save enough money to get back to the hotel for dinner tonight, okay?"

Never having been much of a shopper, Brandon strolled the picturesque street, more interested in its wrought iron signs and attractive window displays than in making any purchases. Happy, jostling tourists crowded the narrow winding avenue, all in holiday mood.

Brandon decided to follow Herta's recommendation and return to the Domplatz. He walked leisurely up the hill and entered the Cathedral to admire once more its ornate Baroque interior. As he examined the elaborately detailed gilt and marble, he noticed a familiar figure standing nearby. It was Father Hochburg, the priest he had first seen when he boarded their plane back in Boston.

Approaching the cleric, who was engrossed in inspecting the magnificent altar, Brandon intruded, "Pardon me, Father. I'm Brandon St. Clair. We're in the same tour group, but I haven't had a chance to get acquainted with you yet."

Father Hochburg extended his hand, his face creased in a broad smile, a look of genuine warmth and welcome in his eyes.

"Hello, Brandon. Of course I recognize you. I'm very happy to get to meet you personally."

Brandon returned the solid handshake. "This is some place of worship, isn't it? Or do you have one as elaborate back home?"

Father Hochburg chuckled, "I'm afraid not. Actually, my church is a small, simple one. But my parishioners make up for it by being such terrific people."

"That's good to hear. Where are you located?"

"On the outskirts of Boston." The priest chuckled again. "I know what you're thinking: How did someone named 'Hochburg' end up in such an Irish community? I'll admit it took them a while to get used to me, but we get along exceptionally well now."

"Maybe you should have changed your name to 'O'Hochburg'. They might have taken to you sooner."

Father Hochburg burst into a hearty laugh. "You may be right, Brandon. But on this trip I plan to have a good time getting acquainted with the German part of my heritage. This is a lovely city, don't you think?"

Brandon agreed whole-heartedly. They strolled slowly from the Cathedral to the massive, ornate fountain in the square. Finding seats at one of the outdoor tables, they continued their dialogue.

"Are you affiliated with any particular church, Brandon?"

"Not really. My parents were members of the Presbyterian Church, but we didn't attend very often." Brandon felt a sharp pang as memories of his parents flooded back. He paused briefly before continuing. "I guess over the years I just kind of developed my own ideas of what religion is."

"What do you mean?" Father Hochburg was curious.

"Well, I've always considered myself to be a very spiritual person, but not a very religious one. Does that make sense?"

"I suppose, in a way. Tell me more."

Brandon took a deep breath. "In your religious studies, Father, didn't you find that each of the major religions is based on the teachings of one outstanding person? That's right, isn't it? For Christianity, there was Jesus; for the Muslim faith, Mohammed; for the Hindu faith, Gautama; for Buddhists, the Buddha, and so on."

"Yes, that's true. And of course there were many others. But what's the point you're getting at?" Father Hochburg looked quizzically at the younger man.

"Let me ask you a question first, Father. Are the basic teachings of each of these men all that different?"

The priest thought for a bit, then responded, "Hmmm, that's a good question. They all do have very similar basic beliefs: Love thy neighbor, the brotherhood of mankind, doing good to others, charity, kindness, tolerance. Maybe the Golden Rule sums it up best."

"That's my point, exactly, Father," Brandon broke in with enthusiasm. "They all taught goodness and kindness. But what happened when their followers tried to put those teachings into actual practice?"

"That's *always* the hard part. Preaching is a lot easier than practice."

"So what happened to the *teachings*? I think they've been mostly ignored or forgotten. Instead, it seems that each religion has turned to worshipping its Great *Teacher*, rather than following the teachings that were its foundation. It's a lot easier to set up *rules* for worship than it is to do what the teachers were really talking about: Love your enemies, turn the other cheek, things like that. Wouldn't you agree?"

"Yes, but rules are necessary for any organization."

Brandon pressed his point, "What if the rules become more important than the original purpose of the organization? Were the early Christian churches established to spread the *teachings* of Jesus, or as a place to worship Him? Hasn't *worship* come to be emphasized most because it's so hard to comply with His teachings in the real world?"

"I see what you're getting at," Father Hochburg replied thoughtfully. Then he smiled. "You'd make a fine priest, Brandon. You express your ideas with real fervor."

Brandon laughed lightly. "I guess I do get carried away. But it's something I feel very strongly about."

"It's good to see you've given it so much thought."

"I guess that's what I mean when I say I'm a spiritual person. I have a strong personal faith, but it's on my own terms. It seems to me that religion stresses obedience to the *rules* each group has set up, while spirituality encourages us to follow our *own* path of spiritual communion."

Recompense

Father Hochburg got up and placed his hand on Brandon's shoulder. "You're going to be okay, I can see that. I'd like to keep our discussion going, but we'd better head back to our hotel, don't you think? We sure wouldn't want to miss our dinner." He chuckled. "I hope we can talk some more another time."

"I'd like that. There are lots of ideas I'd like to run by you."

"Saints presarve us!" rejoined the priest in his best Irish brogue. They made their way slowly down the hill, still engaged in pleasant conversational exchange.

Chapter V

At dinner that evening, Herta had given the group a preview of the next day's activities. Now they were actually on their way. They were to spend the morning exploring the Salzkammergut, a region east of Salzburg famous for its natural beauty.

The travelers could not have anticipated what lay in store. The autobahn took them past the north shore of a lake called the Attersee, where they turned off to follow the road taking them along the edge of the water for a time before leading deeper into a wooded wonderland. The exquisite tree-studded countryside reminded Brandon of family visits to Muir Woods when he was a boy. He wished fervently that his mother and father could be viewing these breath-taking vistas, as they had planned. A wave of remorse engulfed him. But rather than give in to feelings of loss or guilt, he determined to savor the scenic wonders as though through their eyes.

Their motor coach took them to the small village of Gmunden on the Traumsee, where they stopped for lunch. The restaurant was situated directly on the lakefront, enabling the delighted travelers to view the flower-bordered water as they enjoyed their meal. White swans drifting motionlessly in the aquatic blue further enhanced the visionary splendor.

The return trip continued to reveal the beauties of the Alpine woodlands. Brandon was particularly impressed by the cleanliness of the countryside. Whereas typical American woods were cluttered with dead trees and broken branches, these forest areas were extremely tidy. He asked Herman, who was sitting across the aisle from him, about it.

"Tell me, Herman, how do they keep the woods so clean? They look almost like our parks."

"Yah, you're right, they do a goot job of it here, but there is no secret to it. People chust go in the woods and pick up all the shticks for firewood."

The group made a rest stop at the picturesque little hamlet of St. Gilgen, nestled at the end of Lake Wolfgang. Herta informed them that the village was the birthplace of Mozart's mother, and that it also had an outstanding cemetery. While others waited for snacks or browsed in the quaint shops, Brandon headed for the cemetery. He loved visiting old burial grounds, checking headstones, imagining the lives of the people long departed. This one was unusually charming, an amalgam of flowers and wrought iron markers neatly laid out in the shadow of the basilica. Brandon was both delighted and impressed.

Aboard the motor coach once more, with their bus driver Rudolph expertly negotiating the narrow roads, they looped along much of the shore of the Mondsee before finally returning to the autobahn. For Brandon, the Salzkammergut had more than lived up to its advance billing.

Back in Salzburg, Herta announced that everyone would have "free time" until dinner. However, she had some additional information for them first.

"As you know, this is the city of Mozart, a city of music. I hate to tell you, but it's not quite like the Salzburg Music Festival competition you saw in the 'Sound of Music'. Instead, we have small groups presenting classical music programs in lots of different places around Salzburg."

Then she came to the part that caught Brandon's full attention: "I understand that tonight there will be a chamber group performing music by Mozart in the old Archbishop's palace, the Residenz. Maybe some of you would like to go. You can check with the concierge at our hotel to see if there are any tickets still available."

As soon as Herta finished, Brandon headed straight for the concierge's counter in the lobby.

"Pardon me, but our tour director said you may still have some tickets available for tonight's concert at the Residenz. Am I too late?"

"As a matter of fact, you're not," the concierge informed him. "It's good to see our tourists interested in cultural events, not just in taking home trinkets."

"This must be my lucky day! I never dreamed I'd have a chance to hear Mozart performed, right here in his home town."

The concierge courteously provided Brandon with a ticket, his smile broadening at the generous tip included. As Brandon turned to go, the concierge asked, "You're American, aren't you? I can usually pick out the accents."

Brandon returned to the counter. "Yes, I am. And, by the way, I'm totally intrigued with your city. It must be a great place to live year 'round."

"It is. You should be here for the skiing in winter." He extended his hand. "I'm Karl Mettler."

"Brandon St. Clair."

"Where are you from, Mr. St. Clair?"

"California. San Francisco, actually."

"California!" Karl's eyes widened. "There's a place I've always wanted to visit. Maybe I'd like it as much as you like Salzburg." He laughed.

"I'm sure you would, and I hope you make it. Come look me up when you do. Here's my card. I'm not hard to find."

Karl laughed again. "You may get a surprise. I just might find you." Then he returned to his more formal demeanor. "You'll like the program tonight, I'm sure. They're an outstanding group."

"Thank you, thank you very much. I'm really looking forward to it." The exchange only served to enhance the enchantment he already felt for the city and its people.

Recompense

When Brandon returned to the lobby after dinner on his way to the evening's event, he was surprised to find both Father Hochburg and Miss Margaret Wilson at the concierge's counter. Seeing Brandon approach, Mr. Mettler informed him, "It seems that we have two more tourists interested in good music. These two just took my last tickets for tonight's event. Maybe you wouldn't mind all sharing a cab up to the Residenz."

"Not at all", Brandon answered. "That would be fine with me, if it's all right with these two." He looked from Father Hochburg to Miss Wilson.

"I'd be delighted," responded the priest, good-naturedly. "And between us, I'm sure we can properly escort Miss Wilson."

"That would be most kind of you both," Miss Wilson assented. It was the first time Brandon could remember hearing her speak, other than when she had given her name at the Welcome Dinner. She had a rich, mellow voice that complimented her reserved manner and carriage. Although her features were not what would be considered naturally attractive, she displayed a grace and presence that commanded attention.

While Mr. Mettler called for a taxi, Father Hochburg and Brandon renewed their easy conversational interplay. Miss Wilson remained aloof, standing slightly aside.

"So, you like classical music as well as interesting architecture," the priest began.

"That's right. If you add good food to the mix, it about sums up my major interests."

"Aha! I *knew* there was something about you that I liked from the minute I first saw you. Now, just promise you won't lay any more religious philosophies on me tonight. I'm still analyzing your last dose."

They continued their light-hearted banter until the taxi arrived. Both men turned their attention to Miss Wilson, getting her comfortably seated in the front seat while they climbed into the rear. In a matter of minutes they found themselves back at the Domplatz, following the file of concert-goers headed into the Palace.

It was an impressive old building, dating back to the 1500's, its ornate architecture highlighted by huge works of art~a mix of paintings, tapestries, and statuary. The three made their way up the massive staircase and followed the signs toward the Conference Hall. Miss Wilson led the way, turning at the entryway of the Hall to whisper, "Before Mozart moved to Vienna, he used to conduct concerts here."

"How very appropriate!" Brandon remarked. "It seems like you can still almost sense his presence, right in this room."

As they took their seats and looked around, Brandon's attention was drawn to a vast mural that adorned the ceiling of the room. It was a magnificent painting, depicting the future Alexander the Great as a young man, taming his legendary white horse, Bucephalus. Nudging Father Hochburg, Brandon pointed to the ceiling. The look of appreciation that spread over the priest's genial face matched Brandon's own sense of admiration. Apparently the two had found another area of common interest.

The concert was everything Brandon could have hoped for. The measured cadence of the music, interspersed with Mozart's special light, ephemeral touches, was truly "soul" music for him, harmonizing with his innermost spirit. It brought to his mind once again a quotation credited to Friedrich Nietzche: "Without music, life would have been a mistake."

During intermission, having acquired their glasses of light Austrian wine, the three moved out to the narrow balcony encircling the room. Moonlight reflected from the water playing in the massive fountain below. Beyond could be seen the sparkling lights of the city. It was a magical moment. Softly, as though afraid of intruding on the serenity, Father Hochburg murmured, "God's in his heaven, all's right with the world."

They gazed silently for several moments more, until Father Hochburg excused himself with a whispered, "I'll be back in a minute."

Brandon watched him disappear, then turned to Miss Wilson. "What do you think of the program so far?"

Recompense

"Oh, it's lovely! You were right: it's almost as if Mozart *were* here himself, checking to see that his music is interpreted properly." She gave a light, airy laugh.

"Are you a Mozart fan too?"

"Very much. I enjoy all of his works." She lowered her rich voice to a conspiratorial whisper: "Don't tell the people of Salzburg, but my *real* favorites are the Russian composers. I enjoy their fire and their unpredictability."

Brandon nodded. "I see your point, but there's something about the regularity, the order of the German rhythm that touches my spirit. 'To each his own,' I guess. I remember reading something a man named Galsworthy said: 'By the…composers they love, ye shall know the texture of men's souls.'" With a grin he added, "I hope that's not too sexist."

"Not at all. I absolutely agree! Anyway, I'm certainly glad I didn't miss this experience. Did you notice the works of art everywhere? I wish I could take some of them home with me."

"Does that mean you're an art collector? I thought you must be a photographer from the way you handle your camera."

Miss Wilson responded with another of her tinkling laughs. "Actually, I'm neither of those, although I thoroughly enjoy capturing impressions of people and places on film. What I really do is manage a small collection of art works, one we wish we could afford to expand."

"Sounds interesting. Where do you work?"

" Have you heard of the Shelbourne Museum in upstate Vermont?" Brandon shook his head. "I'm not surprised," Miss Wilson went on. "You're from the West Coast, aren't you? You probably don't know about our 'living history' museum. What we have is really a cross-section of early Americana~homes, barns, a grist mill, a light-house, even an old lake steamer from that era. And in the main house we have a small collection of art, with some fine pieces~including some by Grandma Moses. That's what I look after."

"I'd certainly like to see that sometime."

"I hope you'll pay us a visit," Miss Wilson's response was sincere. "My favorite artists are the early Americans, especially some of the 'anonymous' ones, and others like Edward Hicks. They painted exactly what they saw: the real world. They may not have been as skilled, but they had a freedom of spirit that many of the others lack."

"Does that help explain why you also like the Russian composers best~their freedom of spirit?"

Miss Wilson broke into another of her distinctive laughs. "You're quite perceptive, aren't you? But I'll have to plead guilty. Although I enjoyed the art at the Pinakothek in Munich, for instance, I really wish this trip could have taken us to Vienna. They have the most fabulous collection of Brueghels at the Kunsthistorisches Museum there, I've been told. Now Brueghel was an artist who could portray life as he saw it."

"Is that what brought you on this trip, Miss Wilson, the opportunity to visit art museums?"

"Only partly. And my friends call me Margaret, not 'Miss Wilson'".

"Thank you, Margaret. So what's your *real* reason for being here?"

"Why, the Oberammergau Passion Play. It's a once-in-a-lifetime opportunity. Ever since I first read about it, I knew I had to get to Oberammergau." She stopped, as though perplexed, then added quietly, "And you know, I'm not exactly sure *why* I felt so strongly. I just knew I had to see that play."

Once again Brandon felt the familiar chill. He glanced at Margaret, momentarily unable to formulate any words. What was this grand, irresistible attraction of Oberammergau? His mind raced, trying to find some key, some element of commonality, that would help him make sense of this ongoing chain of experiences. A sharp flash of headache pain, one that usually foreshadowed a serious episode, hit his left temple. But this time it passed as quickly as it had come.

Recompense

Relieved, Brandon drew in a deep breath and let it out slowly. He saw that Margaret was looking at him, curiosity and concern on her face.

They were interrupted by Father Hochburg's hurried return. "We'd better get back inside," he announced. "The orchestra is back on stage. The second part of the program is about to begin."

Chapter VI

As much as the travelers had enjoyed Salzburg, Herta informed them it was time to move ahead with their itinerary. Today, she said, the motor coach would take them to Innsbruck.

Along the way, they were to make two stops at points of special interest. The first would be at Herrenchiemsee, one of "Mad King Ludwig's" fabulous castles. "It's not officially part of the tour," Herta explained, "but this quick visit will enable you to see *all* of the young king's extravagant estates. We'll be seeing the others later on our way to Oberammergau."

The second stop would be at the former vacation retreat of Adolf Hitler~his infamous "Wolf's Lair" near Berchtesgaden. Herta was careful to point out: "This visit is in no way intended to 'honor' the former dictator, who represents only a deep moral embarrassment for most present-day Germans. Rather, the purpose is to allow you to observe the vistas of a truly spectacular section of the Alpine Highway."

To reach Herrenchiemsee Castle required that their coach leave the motorway for a short scenic detour to the lake. There, on an island near the western shore of Chiemsee, they could see what appeared to be a smaller replica of Louis XIV's magnificent palace at Versailles. As Herta explained in her commentary, "Young King Ludwig was once a guest at the elegant home of the French 'Sun King' and determined that he, too, should have a palace of similar grandeur. The only problem was the 'Mad King' ran out of money before he could complete his ambitious project and died before his dream could be realized."

Recompense

It was still an impressive sight, including a duplication of the grandiose Hall of Mirrors. As he wandered through the manicured gardens, Brandon could not help but theorize: Did this palace, in a way, reflect the psyche of the German people~or at least that of their leadership? Historically, he knew, France had long been acknowledged as a primary power among European nations, and in the minds of the French, would *always* remain preeminent. At the time Herrenchiemsee was built, Germany had only recently become unified as a nation. A people with tremendous pride but with a divided and disparate history needed *something* to weld together its "volk". However, symbols such as this copy-cat palace had proved not to be enough. It had taken someone like a Hitler, infusing the Germans with his theories that they were a "master race", to overcome the long-standing feelings of international inferiority. It also proved to be a high price to pay for national pride.

When they resumed their journey after this brief stop, Rudolph leaned toward Brandon, who was seated on the front row as part of their regular seat rotation: "Now we'll find out if I can drive this thing or not." The road became a narrow winding ribbon filled with hairpin turns, but it also took them through scenic wonders that none would have dared to miss. Rudolph negotiated the curves expertly, and each turn revealed new panoramas that brought exclamations of amazement from the entranced visitors.

Arriving at last at Berchtesgaden, the group exited the bus for a short break before continuing up the incredibly steep grade to Obersalzberg, set high in the mountains overlooking the valley below. This had been the site of the "Wolf's Lair", once a showplace of the Nazi domain. Now all that remained, aside from a small restored hotel, was the rubble left by the devastating bombing inflicted by the Allies. Brandon felt absolutely no remorse as he surveyed the destruction. He did, however, pick up a fragment of brick from the rubble to keep as a remembrance of the dangers of national pride run amok.

Next the group boarded the local shuttle to proceed even farther up the Kehlstein. The small road clinging precariously to the sheer sides of the mountain left the passengers at once terrified and awe-struck. At the end of the road, their final step was an elevator ride to the summit, site of the infamous "Eagle's Nest" never actually utilized to any degree by Hitler. It was an unbelievable experience, leading to a near-unanimous response: "Look at that view! It makes all of the effort worthwhile!"

The return trip found the group in a subdued mood, still digesting the sights and the significance of what they had seen. Brandon felt as though he had stood at a virtual "crossroads" of history, in which humanity had been forced to make the sanguinary choice between authoritarian oppression or faith in the potential of the individual. It reminded him once more of just how fragile the "progress" of civilization could be.

The quiet persisted as their coach made its way back along the Alpine Highway to its junction with the road to Innsbruck. But by the time they reached this popular Austrian tourist stop on the Inn River, the group had regained much of its customary good humor. This was fortunate, because the evening's agenda included dinner and entertainment at a local Bierkeller, or beer cellar, where a celebratory mood was the norm. The exuberant yodeling and the shoe-slapping, wood-chopping dances soon drew the audience into active participation. Once again, one of the most energetic polka enthusiasts proved to be Herman, who appeared to be totally in his element.

Following a particularly lively dance, Herman came over to where Brandon and Father Hochburg were seated, chatting. Herman's face was flushed, his breath came in gasps, but the large stein of beer he carried seemed to have enhanced his courage and he wore a broad smile.

"Herman, you're a natural at this, aren't you? You looked good out there," Brandon greeted him.

"Ach, yah, this is my kind of dance. None of that fancy stuff for me. Why don't you come try it?"

Recompense

〇つ

Brandon gave a short laugh, "Not on your life! I know my weaknesses, and dancing is certainly one of them."

"You could do it, Brandon. Just give a hop and a skip in time to the music, that's all."

Brandon laughed again. "No, I think I'll just keep watching. It's safer for everyone that way."

"Anyway," Herman went on, wiping his damp forehead with a large blue handkerchief and taking another long draught of his beer, "it's nice to be so close to home, isn't it?"

"What do you mean?" Brandon asked, sincerely puzzled.

"Why, we'll be soon back home in Oberammergau."

"Oberammergau? Why do you call that 'back home'?"

Herman paused, a look of candid surprise in his eyes, as though he too wondered why he had made such a statement. His jovial face reddened. Looking around self-consciously, he stammered, "Ach, I guess it's because I'll be soon seeing again my uncle. Yah, that must be it." With that he turned quickly and retreated to the dance floor.

But for Brandon, the exchange renewed all of the questions that had been bothering him and that he had tried to put out of his mind. Was there really some sort of tie, some association, with this village that everyone kept talking about? Upon what could it be based? Was he only *imagining* the feelings of a psychic "bond"?

His thoughts were interrupted by Father Hochburg. "What was that all about, Brandon?"

"I'm really not sure," Brandon mused. He was silent for a time, then turned to look intently at the priest. "Father, why do some people on this trip seem to be so familiar? It's as if somehow we already *know* each other. But how could that possibly be? And what's so special about Oberammergau that I don't understand? What am I missing here?"

Father Hochburg peered sharply at his agitated companion, surprised at the forcefulness of his queries. He hesitated a moment, then looked directly into Brandon's eyes and murmured softly, "Don't you *know*, Brandon?" With that, as though catching himself, he rose quickly. "Time to get another beer," he said and moved away.

More confused than ever, Brandon sat alone at the long table, deep in thought. Nothing was making sense. Perhaps when we finally get to Oberammergau, he told himself, I'll be able to figure this all out. Now, he only wanted to get back to the hotel.

For the first time since the tour had begun, Brandon spent a restless night, his sleep broken by the speculations of an overactive mind. He got up early to prepare for the day and went down to breakfast.

By now, the tour group had become a rather close-knit family, courteous and respectful of each other's time and thus careful to remain on schedule. The exception was still the Grossfeldt family, who seemed determined to remain a separate entity apart from the rest. This was at least partially due, Brandon was sure, to the reaction of the other tour members to the behavior of the Grossfeldt children. They appeared to be obnoxious almost by design.

This was pointedly reinforced at breakfast that morning. Arriving early, Brandon noted that the only other travelers from their group already present were the Grossfeldts. After selecting his food from the ample buffet, Brandon decided to join the family at their table to see if he couldn't break through their reserve. As he approached, however, he was greeted with hostile glares from the children, followed by a continuation of their incessant bickering and complaining.

"Mom, make Eloise move over," the boy whined in his usual petulant tones. "She's getting her stuff in my way."

"Oh, shut up, Alan," his sister responded, punching his shoulder and sticking out her tongue.

"Stop it, both of you!" Mrs. Grossfeldt intervened. Her comment was completely disregarded, as usual.

"I don't like this cereal," Alan continued. "I want Frosted Flakes. Doesn't this dumb place have any Frosted Flakes?"

"Just be quiet and eat your food," Mr. Grossfeldt said, not bothering to look up from his plate.

"But I don't like this stuff. Make them get me some Frosted Flakes."

"You big baby, Alan, " Eloise cut in. "How would you like to have to eat these goopy scrambled eggs Mom put on my plate? Just shut up!"

"I told you both to stop that," Mrs. Grossfeldt repeated. Again she was thoroughly ignored.

Brandon had heard enough. Maybe he didn't want to get better acquainted with this family after all. He smiled and nodded to the Grossfeldts as he walked on to a more peaceful table by the window.

Despite the unpleasant beginning, the day proved to be a tourist's delight. The City Guide who joined them for their excursion took them first to the site of the 1964 and 1976 Olympics. The long stairway to the top of the ski jump was a challenge, but was made more than worthwhile as they viewed the city spread out below them.

"Look down there," the guide pointed out. "That's Wilten Abbey. I hope some of you get a chance to go inside later on, and also to check the little cemetery nearby."

Next, their guide directed Rudolph to drive the coach slowly down Maria-Theresien Strasse, the historic heart of Innsbruck. They stopped often to absorb the sights of this charming city. St. Anne's Column, rising high above the avenue and silhouetted against the mountains in the background, was perhaps the city's most notable landmark.

Another attraction, much more romanticized, was the "Little Golden Roof", a gilded canopy attached to the front of a stolid former palace. Their guide gave them some background:

"The 'Little Golden Roof' was added to this building by Emperor Maximilian. See that balustrade on the balcony below it? Those woodcuts on the balustrade show the Emperor with each of his two wives. Now," she added with a slight air of superiority, "some people, including some of our less-informed City Guides, still insist that the roof was actually built by Duke Friedrich the Penniless and was covered with gold coins to prove he really wasn't poor. It's a cute story, but it just isn't true."

Their group greeted this explanation with amused chuckles. Brandon concluded that the latter version, whether accurate or not, *was* more memorable.

The highlight of the day, however, came for Brandon when the group was given "free time" until their departure later that afternoon. He remembered having read in a travel book about an Old Innsbruck restaurant that had been frequented by notable personalities over the years, including King Gustav of Sweden. It was called the "Goldener Adler", or Golden Eagle, and Brandon was determined to find it and have lunch there.

As it turned out, the directions he had jotted down were perfect, quite different from the "you can't miss it" type he frequently encountered. Just around the corner from the ornately decorated pink Heblinghaus and down the street from the "Little Golden Roof," he found it. Sure enough, the huge marble plaque next to the doorway identified some of the establishment's most famous guests. There was the name of King Gustav, prominently displayed. Among the many other names, beginning with the King of Tunis in the 1540s, Brandon noted the Italian composer Nicolo Pagannini. The latest entry, the King of Thailand and his Princess, had dined there in 1982.

Brandon went inside, filled with a special sense of satisfaction at having found the place. Further heightening his pleasure was the quality of the food, featuring stag, served by a pleasant young waitress who introduced herself as Gretchen. His table next to a window on the second floor enabled him to observe tourists browsing busily below. As he savored his lunch, Brandon gazed around appreciatively, thinking, Wow, who'd have guessed I'd ever be having an experience like this!

Recompense

❧

After lunch, Brandon spent time leisurely exploring a small floral garden nearby, then started back toward the hotel. The growing sense of anticipation he felt building within him was due, he knew, to only one factor: the group was about to depart for Oberammergau! At last he would be closer to the source of events that had proved so baffling! As he walked along, deep in thought, Brandon muttered quietly to himself, "I wonder what we'll find there. Could we really be 'going home' again, like Herman said?"

Chapter VII

Everyone in the group arrived on time for the 2:00 o'clock departure, except, as usual, for the Grossfeldts. The tour members waited as patiently as possible, chatting casually, but Brandon could detect an undercurrent of growing annoyance at one more delay. Finally, the family appeared, Mr. Grossfeldt half-dragging young Alan, who was still protesting loudly.

"Why are you making me go? I want to hear the band some more."

"Be quiet and get on the bus," his father ordered. Mrs. Grossfeldt appeared genuinely chagrined.

Underway at last, they made good time as they left Austria. Shortly they entered the colorful German border town of Mittenwald. Heavy traffic forced Rudolph to proceed slowly down the main street, enabling the travelers to exclaim over the artistically decorated houses lining the thoroughfare. Brandon remembered reading that the poet Goethe had once described Mittenwald as a "living picture-book," and decided that, at least in his estimation, the town readily matched that depiction.

From there it was only a short distance to Garmisch-Partenkirchen, jointly-governed cities that had once been a Winter Olympics site and still formed one of Bavaria's most popular ski resorts. Garmisch in particular, with its Old Town center and decorated buildings, insisted on maintaining many of its Alpine traditions. This year, Herta told them, both towns would also serve as stopping-places for part of the flood of tourists coming to see the performances at Oberammergau. The superb setting in the Bavarian Alps, along with its accessibility from Munich, made this an attractive spot for the "overflow".

Rudolph turned off the main road briefly and stopped their coach at a flower-decked corner restaurant, as Herman directed him to do. It was here that Herman was to meet his uncle. As he left the bus, he waved to the group and proclaimed, "Don't worry, I'll see you all at the Passion Play." The passengers called out cheery farewells, mingled with shouts of "Have fun, Herman." Obviously, the affable little man had become a favorite with almost everyone.

As they got under way once more, Brandon began to experience a rising sense of excitement. The next stop would be Oberammergau! At last they would reach the destination that seemed to engender such powerful feelings of anticipation. What unexpected secrets did it hold? Would it finally provide some answers, or would there only be additional questions? His curiosity was tinged with nervousness as they neared the awaited goal.

The same sense of expectancy seemed to have permeated the rest of the travelers as well. It was reflected in the nervous, galvanic chatter that rose and spread through the bus like an electrical charge. Obviously, Brandon was not alone in his speculations about what lay ahead for them in Oberammergau.

As their coach entered the village, Herta directed Rudolph to proceed as slowly as traffic would permit, explaining, "Just ahead you'll see some good examples of what makes Oberammergau such an attractive place. On your right is the 'Hansel and Gretel' house, while across the street on your left is the 'Rotkappchenhaus' or 'Red Ridinghood House'. These are only two of the many 'painted houses' for which the town is famous, in addition to its Passion Play."

Brandon constantly shifted his watchful gaze so as not to miss any-thing. It was a truly picturesque spot, he noted. A wealth of handsome, intricately-painted murals lavishly adorned the exteriors of many of the structures, enhancing their charm, as did the traditional flower boxes filled with brightly colored geraniums. Religious themes vied with Alpine and story-book scenes to give the streets a remarkable make-believe atmosphere.

Rudolph maneuvered the coach expertly into the widened area in the street alongside the Hotel Alte Post, where his passengers were to disembark before he moved the vehicle to the bus park outside the village center. This would be their home for the next three nights.

On their way into town, Herta had already informed the group, "In the past, our tour company has often used the Hotel BØld, because Mr. and Mrs. Hans are always such gracious hosts. However, this year they were completely booked almost two years in advance, so we were really extremely fortunate that our company was able to take advantage of a late cancellation at the Hotel Alte Post instead. You see, this is by far the oldest hotel in town, built back in 1612, even before the plague came to Oberammergau. It's been in continuous operation ever since. And I'm sure you'll appreciate the attention the current proprietors, the Preizingers, always give their guests as well."

A radiant pastel sky filled with wispy clouds catching the last lingering rays of the setting sun greeted the travelers as they stepped from the bus. Could this be an omen, Brandon wondered? Still, there was no hint so far that this town would be notably different from others they had visited, and a vague sense of disappointment swept over him.

Then he turned, and the unexpected view brought an involuntary gasp of surprise. There it was: a perfect picture-postcard. Framed by flower-decked shops on each side of the street, directly before him appeared the elaborately decorated building whose picture he had come across in the travel brochure his parents had so carefully included with their tour tickets. The entire upper story of the structure was covered by a huge mural, one side depicting Christ on the cross, the other what appeared to be a gathering of religious leaders proclaiming the significance of His death and Resurrection. Behind the building, in the distance, could be seen the brooding, curved prominence of a mountain, the same dominant peak that Brandon remembered he had seen in the little village in his reverie! At its summit, a solitary cross reflected the twilight sun.

Involuntarily, Brandon halted, drawing in his breath. It was a truly splendid scene, in spite of the disquietude he felt at its familiarity. Turning to Mrs. Scheer, he exclaimed almost reverently, "Have you ever seen anything more perfect? It seems to sum up the whole Oberammergau aura, doesn't it?"

"You're right, Brandon! That's got to be one of the most enchanting sights I've seen." She paused momentarily, then added, "I think Oberammergau is going to meet *all* of our expectations." She smiled softly, leaving Brandon to ponder the implication of her words.

At dinner that evening, Brandon asked Herta if she knew the name of the distinctive mountain that seemed to serve as such a guardian for the village. "Oh yes, that's the Kofelberg," she informed him. "It's the tallest peak in the surrounding Oberammergau Alps, and looks almost like its part of the town by now." Brandon could only smile in agreement.

After dinner, Herta reviewed their itinerary for the remaining tour time. "Tomorrow," she explained, "we'll spend the day visiting the exotic Royal Castles of 'Mad King' Ludwig. I think you'll be suitably impressed. But the following day you'll experience an adventure I'm sure you will never forget, the event you all came so many miles to see. We'll spend the whole day attending a presentation of the historic Passion Play."

Her enthusiasm carried over to the tour members, and comments of "I can hardly wait!" and "I still can't believe it!" sounded through the room. For Brandon, the intentness only magnified the mystique that had arisen around this entire episode.

Herta continued her commentary: "Following that, there will be one more 'free day' in Oberammergau, time for you to explore the village on your own and enjoy its many attractions~the shops, wood-carving factories, the church, the cemetery, little streets, whatever you find most interesting. I think the day will be a fitting 'grand finale' for our tour, after which Rudolph will take us all back to Munich for your return flights home."

Excitement was at a high level as they set out the next morning. Their first stop was Linderhof Castle, less grand than its nearby neighbors and hence sometimes overlooked. Set in the Ammergau Alps, it again reflected admiration for French influences and royal personages, though it fell somewhat short in French architectural opulence .

Most impressive, in Brandon's estimation, were the gardens. Very formally laid out in the Italian style, they carried the eye upward to the Moorish Pavilion, reminiscent of the grand Taj Mahal. According to Herta, this elaborate edifice had served as a grandiose "tea house" for Ludwig II and his guests. When Brandon made his way up the pathway past the elegant floral exhibitions and cascading fountains to the Pavilion itself, he was rewarded with a breathtaking panoramic view of the gardens and castle below.

Equally fascinating was the Grotto, a huge cavern which Ludwig had ordered carved into a solid hillside rock. "This was designed as a subterranean setting where operas and other extravaganzas could be performed," Herta told them. "Notice, it even comes complete with an artificial lake and a shell-shaped boat. But would you believe, only *one* performance ever actually took place here?" As he gazed around in awe, Brandon was coming to understand more and more how Ludwig II had earned the sobriquet "Mad King."

When Herta rounded up the group to move on to their next stop, they discovered that Alan Grossfeldt was missing.

Recompense

"He was with us in the gift shop. I told him to stay right there, but when I looked around, he was gone, and now we can't find him," Mrs. Grossfeldt explained, near tears.

"If you hadn't kept squabbling about what souvenir we should buy, you could have watched him," Mr. Grossfeldt accused. "He must have wandered outside while you weren't looking."

Both parents began rushing about the area, calling frantically, "Alan, where are you?" Eloise sat pouting on the bus, muttering threats and refusing to help.

Brandon and Father Hochburg quickly joined the search, methodically revisiting the areas the group had been to earlier. Deep in the Grotto, they found him. He was standing by the lake, idly throwing small rocks into the water, one after another.

"Alan!" Brandon called. "Thank God, you're safe! Your parents were really worried about you."

"So? Go tell them I'm not leaving here 'till I get a ride on that boat."

"I'm afraid that's not possible, son," Father Hochburg explained. "That isn't a real boat, and besides, it's past time to be going on to the next castle."

"I'm not your son, and I want a ride on that boat," Alan screamed, jumping up and down. "You can't make me go. You're not my boss."

Grasping the boy's chubby arms firmly, one on each side, Brandon and Father Hochburg led him, still protesting loudly, from the Grotto and back toward their waiting bus. As they approached, the anxious Grossfeldts rushed to meet them, relief and frustration intermingled in their frenetic exclamations.

"They wouldn't let me ride the boat," Alan whined. "They hurt my arms, too, real bad! Get a policeman and arrest them, okay? They're mean!"

Despite Alan's protestations, Mrs. Grossfeldt was profuse in her thanks to the two men. Everyone boarded the bus to cheers from the waiting passengers, and finally the group was on its way.

As they continued through the wooded vistas, Herta informed them, "Since we're running a little late, I think we should concentrate on only one of the remaining Royal Castles, Neuschwanstein. It's by far the most photographed, so it will be the most familiar. And you've all seen the replica at Disneyland, haven't you?"

When they arrived at Neuschwanstein, one glance convinced Brandon that Herta had made a wise choice. There was truly a "fairy-tale" atmosphere about the castle, its fortress-like massiveness broken by the intricacy of its towers, battlements, and crenelations.

"Wow! Isn't this something?" Brandon heard Father Hochburg remark. "It certainly lives up to its reputation!"

Once inside, the visitors gaped in wonder. Here was a wealth of gilt and marble, inter-mingled with rich tapestries, paintings, and statuary, that lavishly enhanced its illusory atmosphere. Further, the palace was pervaded by an ever-present swan motif, from which it had drawn its name. As the group moved from room to room, it became apparent why the "Mad King's" castle-building had so thoroughly depleted the national treasury.

Perhaps the most awe-inspiring room, the group agreed, was the Royal Hall. It looked as though it could have been designed for a Byzantine potentate. Rows of columns ringed the room on two levels, connected by Moorish-style arches. Bright, colorful paintings completely covered the walls behind the columns. Above, another series of huge arches, framing more elaborate paintings, carried the whole theme upward to form a vaulted ceiling. And since construction of the room had been blocked by impenetrable rock, it was not built in a rectangular shape, but instead in the form of a trapezoid. To complete the extravagant tableau, an enormous chandelier hung from the ceiling. It could be lowered or raised by a complex system of ropes and pulleys so that its candles could be lighted or extinguished.

Recompense

Wandering about the upper floors provided the visitors an opportunity to view the exquisite lake-studded, wooded countryside in which Neuschwanstein Castle was set. Brandon walked out onto the balcony, and before him appeared the Pallat waterfall. Above the falls arched the graceful Marienbròcke. Looking in another direction through a castle window, he caught a glimpse of Hohenschwangau Castle, their next destination, deep in the Alpine forest. Everything combined to enhance the aura of unreality.

Margaret Wilson was everywhere, Brandon noted, trying to capture the essence of the magnificent structure through the lens of her camera. "You're having a field day here, aren't you, Margaret?" he commented as she passed. "I've never seen anything like it! I only hope some of my shots will do it justice." She moved on quickly, in search of one last perfect photo before time ran out.

When Herta indicated that it was time to resume their journey, the group left the castle with sincere reluctance. It was hard for Brandon not to be a bit resentful that Alan's little escapade had cost them some of their valuable excursion time.

Hohenschwangau Castle, the last of the royal residences and an attractive structure in its own right, could not match Neuschwanstein's dramatic appeal, in Brandon's opinion. The visit became almost perfunctory, although the group did find King Ludwig's bedchamber interesting, with its ceiling designed like a night sky, including stars that could actually be lighted. When the time came to move on, however, they were all ready to go, well saturated with castles for the present.

Rudolph proposed that, instead of returning along the same road by which they had come, they follow a slightly longer but different route on the trip back to Oberammergau. After consulting the group and checking the time, Herta agreed. Again, flexibility proved to be a bonus. They now drove through the stunning scenic region that they had viewed earlier from the castle, as they made their way through the Fussen countryside.

But the real highlight came when they reached the Wieskirche, the "church in the meadow," built on a low hill some distance from the surrounding Bavarian Alps. As they walked up the pathway and entered this small pilgrimage church, it seemed they had been transported to another world. Whereas the Royal Castles appeared to be dedicated to opulent ostentation, this quiet sanctuary reflected grandness tempered by tasteful dignity. At the same time, it was without doubt the most elegant, ornate church Brandon had ever been in~a blending of white and gold, with breath-taking ceiling frescoes and organ choir loft, that represented the epitome of the pretentious Rococo style, yet achieved a remarkable unity and harmony.

Brandon approached Father Hochburg, who was gazing at the surroundings in awe. "Well, what do you think? Each church seems to get more elaborate than the last one, doesn't it?"

"I'll say! But I think it's going to be awfully hard to top this."

When they returned to their coach, Brandon stopped to say, "Rudolph, thanks so much for suggesting we take this 'detour.' I wouldn't have missed this for anything."

"You're most welcome," Rudolph replied, a smile of deep pleasure creasing his face. "Visitors to our country sometimes get so busy with their shopping or accommodations that they miss our real treasures. I'm happy to see you appreciate them."

With the diversions of the day behind them and the return to Oberammergau ahead, the travelers began to feel once more a resurgence of the anticipation that had infected them on their arrival the previous day. It was a prospect filled with a blending of eagerness and suspense, and now there would be no further delays. Tomorrow, at last, they would actually witness the Passion Play!

CHAPTER VIII

"Good morning, Mrs. Scheer," Brandon greeted his traveling companion cheerfully as he neared her table in the breakfast area. She was the only tour member already there, and he had not found many opportunities recently to chat with her.

She looked up quickly as he spoke, and her face brightened with a warm smile. "Why, good morning, Brandon. It's so nice to see you. Won't you please join me?" She indicated a chair across the table. "It looks like we're the early birds today, doesn't it?"

"Yes, it does. I woke up early and couldn't get back to sleep, so I thought I might as well get started on the day."

Mrs. Scheer laughed. "The same thing happened to me. I think we're all pretty excited about today~finally seeing the Passion Play, after all this time."

"I know *I* am," Brandon replied. He became serious for a moment before continuing. "And you know, I'm still not sure *why*. There's just something about this whole situation that I don't understand." He shook his head, genuinely perplexed.

Adding to his confusion was a recurrence of the airy but unmistakable aroma of fresh baked cookies wafting through the air. He had come to associate this with Mrs. Scheer's presence, but he still couldn't explain it. He looked around the room, and saw that cookies were definitely not part of the breakfast menu. Yet, the scent was there. Somehow, there had to be a connection.

Mrs. Scheer broke into his speculation. "For me," she said slowly, as though deep in thought, "I guess there was never a question of *why* I wanted to be here, only *if* and *when* I'd finally be able to."

"What do you mean?"

"I've heard of the Oberammergau Passion Play for as long as I can remember. My grandmother attended a performance when she was a young girl, before the family came to America, and she always told me how wonderful it was. It really made a lasting impression on her. My mother had hoped to take me to see it sometime, but she was never able to come up with the extra money after Father died. So all she could do was keep talking about it." Mrs. Scheer wiped a tear from the corner of her eye. "I guess I'm really doing this as much for her as for myself," she added quietly.

Brandon reached over and gently patted her hand. "I'm so glad that you were able to make it, to fulfill your dream. That's great!" He felt tears welling in his own eyes at the reminder of his parents, and their inability to experience what had obviously also been a dream for them.

"Thank you, Brandon," Mrs. Scheer said, regaining her customary buoyant composure. "Anyway, I hope it lives up to the expectations I've built up over all these years."

"I'm just sure it will. I guess I don't really have any special expectations myself, because for me this was such a last-minute decision. As a matter of fact, I have no idea whatsoever what's going to happen, or how the whole Play is even presented. Do you have any clues that might help?"

Mrs. Scheer smiled and seemed to take on a special glow. "I might be able to help a little, based on what Grandmother used to tell us. Of course, that was long, long ago, and a lot may have changed since then. But I think they've tried to keep the performances mostly in the same tradition."

"If you could tell me some of what she told you, that would be a great start."

Recompense

✑

"Well, to begin with, I hope you've been practicing your German, because you're going to be hearing about five and a half hours of it, from what I understand."

"Wow! Five and a half hours? I haven't used my German since I graduated from college, and that was longer ago than I care to think about."

"You'll be fine. Lots of the audience probably doesn't know any German at all, but they can still follow the story through the pageantry. Besides, I'm told you can buy a little book with the entire dialogue in English. That's what I plan to do."

"Good! Thanks for the tip. That should help make it more understandable."

"And the story is a familiar one~unless, of course, you never went to Sunday school," Mrs. Scheer laughed brightly.

"Oh, I know the story," Brandon responded, joining in the laughter. "But five and a half hours still seems like a long time."

"It takes that long to get from Christ's entry into Jerusalem through His Crucifixion, Resurrection, and Glorification. They take their story-telling seriously here."

"Who plays all the parts? Do they bring in professional actors and actresses? And where do they get all of the people to play the seventeen hundred different roles I read were involved?"

"Oh, that's one of the best things about it. All of the performers~Jesus, Mary, Judas, Pontius Pilate, every one of them~have to be residents of Oberammergau, either born in the village or have lived here for many years. They work here year 'round, too, in the shops and stores. But I've heard that competition to play the main characters can really get heated. It's considered a great honor to play *any* of the parts."

"That's really fascinating. But where do they get enough characters for all of those parts in a town this size?"

"Well, I understand some people do play several different roles, but it still involves a good many of the residents, either as players or in some behind-the-scenes capacity."

Again Brandon reached over to squeeze her hand. "Thank you so much, Mrs. Scheer. You've been a terrific help. It gives me at least some perspective on what's ahead."

She looked genuinely pleased. "I'm happy to hear that, Brandon. By the way, if you call me 'Louise' it will make me feel less like I've been teaching a class," she chuckled. Her face seemed to take on a special radiance, and the cookie aroma was markedly enhanced.

"Thank you, Louise, I'll like that," He glanced at his watch. "But we'd better get going now, I suppose. Lots of the others have come and gone while we were 'in school'." She smiled affectionately as he headed for the doorway leading back to the hotel.

Before he could make his exit, however, Brandon was halted by a familiar voice.

"Hey, Brandon, goot to see you again," boomed out in Herman's unmistakable tones. He was back to see the Play, as he had promised. Brandon had been afraid the cheery little man might not make it in time, knowing that family visits can often take much longer than planned.

"Hello, Herman," Brandon halted to greet his genial friend. "Glad you made it back. We missed you." He gave Herman's arm a comradely squeeze. "How was your visit with your uncle? Will he be joining us today?"

"Ach no," Herman replied with his usual broad grin. "He saw the Play last month, so you're shtuck with chust me." He gave a hearty laugh.

The air of expectancy was tangible as the group boarded the bus for the short drive to the open-air theater where the Passion Play would be presented. Fortunately, it was a bright, crisp day. Even though it would be a bit cool, they would not have to endure hours of watching the Play in the rain, which Herta had explained was not uncommon at these productions. While there was a roof covering the audience, the performance stage was open to the heavens, giving it a natural, realistic atmosphere.

When they arrived at the drop-off area in front of the theater, Herta led the group toward the large stone-block structure. "They've been very busy renovating the exterior and improving the seating area," she told them. While their reserved seats were part of the tour package, she did have some last minute information for them:

"Your seats are in the center section, on row eleven. That will give you a great view of the stage. And since it's a rather chilly morning, you might want to rent a blanket from one of the booths over there." She indicated an area nearby. "Of course, I understand they've installed a new floor heating system for this year, so maybe you'll be warm enough."

Margaret Wilson raised her hand with a question: "Do you know where we can find the English translation booklets of the dialogue? I was told they were available someplace around here."

"Yes, you can buy them right there near the blankets. You'll have plenty of time before the Play starts."

Louise Scheer looked knowingly at Brandon and smiled. Both went over to pick up booklets as well as blankets. "Better to be well prepared than sorry later, don't you think?" she commented.

"Absolutely! That's the way I always like to operate."

In the flurry of activity to make sure everything was in order, Brandon almost missed a unique work of art nearby. Under a canopy of trees, situated on a large gray rock, was a near life-sized metal statue of Christ, riding on a donkey~reminiscent of His arrival in Jerusalem. Below, water poured from several clefts in the rock~perhaps, Brandon mused, to represent His cleansing power, or the rite of baptism.

Louise Scheer was also studying the figure. "Do you think that water coming from the rock represents the time Moses smote the rock in the wilderness?"

"That's certainly a possibility," Brandon responded, adding that concept to his other theories. He'd have to think more about this later. Whatever the point intended, he knew that the statuary provided an inspirational introduction to the proceedings of the day.

Once inside the huge amphitheater, one that seated an audience of nearly five thousand, they were directed to their seats. Above the stage was a clear blue sky, broken only by an occasional puff of white cloud. Still, the stage and all of its massive sets representing Old Jerusalem had been designed to withstand the elements, so that productions could be held "rain or shine." Brandon was pleased that their day had turned out to be "shine".

Right on time, with customary German punctuality, heralds announced the beginning of the performance. The audience settled back expectantly. Following the introductory portion of the program, a vocal oration spoken in clear, measured German that could be followed readily in the translation booklet, two brief tableaux from the Old Testament were presented. Based on the concepts of old "miracle plays," these tableaux appeared to be designed as reminders that the "Passion" of Christ had long been foretold in Scripture. The program booklet indicated that similar introductions would precede each scene.

Then the drama itself began to unfold. It was an impressive, joyful scene, made even more so by the elegant, colorful costumes. A triumphant Christ entered the city riding on a donkey, while his followers waved majestic palm branches and shouted "Hosannas." The familiar story was brought magnificently to life.

As the Play progressed, Brandon periodically observed his companions. They were all paying rapt attention, caught up in the dramatic portrayals, alternating their concentration between the stage and their translation booklets. Despite the barrier presented by differences of language, every-one appeared to be completely engrossed in the evolving drama. Even the

Recompense

Grossfeldt children were sitting quietly, as though absorbed in a large-screen television program.

The pageant continued its portrayal of the events comprising the last week of the life of Christ. Highlights included His conflict with the High Council, the Last Supper depicting Jesus and the Disciples arrayed as in a Da Vinci painting, followed by Christ's ceremonial washing of the Disciples' feet. From there the group moved to the Mount of Olives, where betrayal by Judas Iscariot led to Christ's arrest.

While he was enjoying the production immensely, Brandon was also beginning to feel what for him was a truly ominous, unwelcome sensation: the first twinges indicating the onset of a major, unrelenting headache. For days, he had delighted in complete freedom from the harsh pain. Now, at what seemed to be a most inopportune juncture, it was returning with a vengeance.

Brandon couldn't determine why. Could it be the intensity of the production that was affecting him? Was it *guilt* that he was somehow "stealing" this unique experience from his parents? Or was it a function of what was occurring around him: the actual playing out of the Passion Play, here in Oberammergau, with all of the attendant mystical and unexplainable episodes that had preceded this moment?

Whatever the cause, Brandon knew from the growing intensity of the torment that this would not be merely a passing episode. He looked around anxiously. All of the others were focused intently on the stage. Shutting his eyes tightly, pressing his fingertips to his temples, moving his head slowly from side to side, he tried to ease the tension, but to no avail.

Just as he felt the pain surge to an almost unendurable peak, it suddenly ebbed. Brandon opened his eyes, blinking, in time to see the characters on stage complete the final actions of the first half of the production. As appreciative applause echoed through the audience, Brandon joined in, thankful that he had survived the initial onslaught. Perhaps moving about, eating lunch, changing his location would help to break the seemingly inevitable pattern of gradually intensifying agony. He could only hope.

"Wasn't that impressive?" Father Hochburg remarked from his seat beside Brandon as the applause died down.

Turning to face the personable cleric, Brandon smiled and responded enthusiastically, "I'll say! I couldn't believe the realism of their presentation. They do live their roles, don't they?"

"They certainly do. You feel almost like you've been transported back in time."

Brandon felt a return of the old chill as the priest uttered these last words. A feeling of foreboding gripped him. Why, he wondered? The words had been spoken innocently enough. Yet, there was something about those words "transported back in time", some intangible deeper meaning, that seemed to foreshadow transcendental events over which Brandon knew he had no control.

A reflexive shiver shook him, and he turned his attention to the audience filing out of the theater, like participants in a slow-motion melodrama. But the promise of a "great German lunch" finally brought him back to reality. He hurried to catch up with the others gathering around Herta, waiting at the pre-appointed meeting-place near the statuary of Christ on the rock. What the remainder of the day would hold he could only wonder.

CHAPTER IX

Herta finally succeeded in rounding up the group members~except for the Grossfeldt children, who had seized on a moment of parental distraction to make their way toward the theater stage, where they were now arguing noisily about what character each would play. A harried usher was trying to explain to them, in German, why they were not allowed to go on stage. Alan was responding with his own demands: "I want to ride the live donkey! You can't tell me what to do. You don't even talk English. I want to ride the donkey!

As Alan's voice increased in stridency, the usher likewise heightened the volume of his German. Eloise's contribution was to interject, "Alan, you big baby!"~also in a tone designed for the largest possible audience. Heads turned to see what was causing all of the commotion.

The noise alerted the Grossfeldt parents as well. Rushing forward, they ordered the two protesting children away from the stage. Then, each firmly grasping one of their offspring by the arm, they led them back to the waiting group.

Herta maintained her usual patient manner. Quickly she explained, "The restaurant where we'll be having lunch isn't far, right across the street, but we all need to arrive promptly, and as a group. We'll have just enough time to get there for our scheduled reservations, and that's important because so many people will be trying to find a place to eat during intermission. So let's all stick together, and follow me."

They arrived at the restaurant, its exterior artistically decorated, colorful flowers blooming in the manicured gardens on either side of the entry. Hurrying inside, they were directed to a separate room where a long table was already set. Their uniformed waiter, who gave his name as Hans, informed them that in the interest of time, the restaurant always served only one menu to large groups. "I hope you will all enjoy your meal," he added in his articulate English.

Their lunches arrived punctually. As his plate was placed before him, Brandon eyed the food with pleasant expectation: tastefully presented, it consisted of cole-slaw, thin slices of pork loin accompanied by baked apple slices, all covered with a light, creamy sauce, plus whole tiny carrots delicately flavored with brown sugar. Complemented by his usual glass of wine, it promised to be a truly delectable repast. For dessert, Hans promised apple-strudel.

Before they could begin, however, they were interrupted once again by Alan Grossfeldt. "I said I wanted French fries," he whined. "I don't like this stuff. You promised I could have French fries!"

Almost as though he had somehow anticipated Alan's ultimatum, Hans appeared with a plate of golden French fries and placed them before the petulant boy. Alan looked genuinely surprised.

His father grumbled, "Now are you satisfied?" and turned to his own plate of food.

"Alan, you big baby!" Eloise contributed.

Mrs. Grossfeldt's face turned red. She reached for a roll and gave her full attention to spreading it with butter.

For Brandon, the first bites of food proved he had assessed correctly. But he had barely begun his meal when, without warning, the headache agony suddenly returned with a vengeance. He put down his fork, closed his eyes tightly, and once again pressed his fingertips hard against his temples. It didn't help. Hoping no one would notice, he kept his eyes lowered as he toyed with his food.

Recompense

⌒

Across the table, Father Hochburg and Margaret Wilson were involved in a spirited discussion, which nevertheless had serious undertones. Margaret was posing a question to which she had obviously given much thought: "Why is it, Father, that women play such a subservient role throughout the Bible."

"What do you mean, 'subservient'?" the clergyman countered, his tone a bit defensive.

"Well, take the play we've been watching, for instance. How many female Apostles were there? How many women on the High Council? And why are references to the Supreme Being always masculine, like 'God the Father'? Why not a Supreme Mother, as many of the ancient religions taught?"

"Whoa! That's not just one question," Father Hochburg replied good-naturedly, "that's a whole theology lecture." He chuckled. "To begin with, though, aren't you forgetting Mary, who certainly plays a prominent role?"

"That's just my point," Margaret came back. "Mary is deeply revered, especially in your church, Father, but she's still limited totally to the 'mother' role. What else do we really know about her, other than that she was the 'Mother of Jesus'? Did she have any hopes or aspirations of her own, as a person, for *herself*? That's never mentioned."

Father Hochburg thought for a moment before responding. "If you want outgoing or heroic women, how about Deborah, or Ruth?"

Margaret remained unconvinced. "All Ruth seemed to be interested in was finding a husband. That's not too 'heroic'. And who really knows much about Deborah? Everyone seems to be a lot more familiar with women like Jezebel, or Delila, or Bathsheba~not exactly my idea of 'role models'."

The cleric raised his hands in mock surrender. "Okay, okay, you've made your point." He laughed and looked across at Brandon. "You're being unusually quiet. Why aren't you helping me out here?"

Brandon raised his eyes, trying to smile through the pain. "I'm getting a kick out of just listening, and I can sure learn a lot more that way than if I'm talking. Besides, I'm liable to be on Margaret's side rather than yours, so I'd better stay quiet."

Father Hochburg looked more closely at the younger man, concerned. "Something's wrong, isn't it, Brandon? Are you feeling all right? You look like you're hurting."

"Oh, just a headache," Brandon said as nonchalantly as he could. "Maybe I'll go find myself an aspirin. Will you excuse me, please? I'll see you back at the theater."

Both Margaret and the priest wished him well. Brandon stopped to inform Herta that he would return to the theater on his own, since the three-hour intermission would allow time to do a little exploring in the village. With her approval, he made his way outside.

Slowly the headache pain began to subside. Breathing deeply in relief, Brandon nevertheless decided to check the nearby shops to see if he could find some pain relievers. It would give him an excuse to see more of Oberammergau.

As he wandered leisurely down the street, he observed that the shops appeared to specialize mostly in wood-carving products rather than in the pain remedy he was seeking. That's all right, he thought. His headache was much better now, and the wood-carvings were more interesting anyway.

Entering one of the shops with an especially attractive window display, Brandon was overwhelmed by both the variety and the quality of the wood-carvings. Row after row of wooden creations greeted him, some done in simple styles, others reflecting the patience and skill of a master craftsperson. Brandon browsed slowly down the rows. He did not normally enjoy shopping, but there was something about the basic naturalness of the wood that fascinated him.

Recompense

One item in particular caught his attention. It was a figurine of the Madonna and Child. Mary was standing with the sleeping infant Jesus cradled gently in her arms, one hand beneath him, the other holding his small leg. Care, concern, and mother-love were combined in the pensive expression on her face. Her head was covered with a shawl, while the rest of her was draped in flowing, intricate folds. The toe of one sandal peeked delicately from beneath the hem of her robe. The whole piece had a quiet dignity, along with a sense of movement that made it seem almost alive.

"You like dot vun?" a heavily accented voice asked from behind him.

Brandon turned. His eyes widened in surprise as he experienced once more the stunning sensation he had first felt when he'd seen Mrs. Scheer and the others on the airplane. He stood frozen, staring at the speaker~bearded, fully costumed, looking as though he had just stepped from the pages of the Bible. Still, the man's eyes held a kind of forlorn wistfulness, until they met Brandon's. Unexpectedly, they then mirrored a surprise equal to his own.

"You're one of the characters from the Passion Play, aren't you?" Brandon asked, still intently inspecting the man.

"Yah, I am," the man responded, smiling. "Can you guess vitch vun?"

Brandon continued his examination. "Why, you're Judas Iscariot. Am I right?"

"Yah, dot's me." The man laughed. "You vas vatching da play pretty goot." He returned Brandon's quizzical look. "But you vas here before, yah? I remember you, I tink."

"No," Brandon shook his head. "This is my first time in Germany." Brandon couldn't help feeling that there was more to the man's familiarity than just the play. "Why do you ask?"

"It's chust dot I tink I see you before," the actor replied in a puzzled tone. He frowned, still staring. Then his face brightened as he added,

"Ach, too many peoples, I guess." He cleared his throat. "You like da Madonna, yah?"

"Oh yes, very much. How much is it?" Brandon took out his wallet and checked the contents. "I just have American dollars. Will that be a problem?"

"No, no, dollars iss goot."

The price was readily agreed upon. As the purchase was being wrapped, they continued their conversation.

"Is it difficult playing the role of Judas?" Brandon asked. "After all, he's not exactly the favorite character in your wonderful Passion Play."

The actor chuckled, "Yah, dot's true. But by now, I'm used to it. I alvays play Yudas, effery time, effery ten years."

"Every time? Why is that? I was told there was lots of competition for each part. You're a fine actor. Why wouldn't you want to try for another role?"

"No, no, I chust play Yudas," the man insisted. "I nefer play annuder part, chust like my fodder. He play Yudas, too, you know, and so dus my grandfodder before him. *Effery* oldest son in da family play Yudas, as long as anyvun remembers. Yah, dis year *my* only son vas sposed to play Yudas, but no, he vants to fly da planes. Next time, he plays Yudas. Ven he qvits da planes, he play Yudas, too. Yah, my family, ve *alvays* play Yudas."

Thoroughly intrigued, Brandon continued to press the point, "But *why?* What is it about the Judas character that so captivates your family?"

"Nudding special. Ve chust play Yudas," the man maintained stubbornly. "It's a madder uf family honor." He halted briefly, his mood darkening, before he added in a low voice, "Unless, uf course, vun leafs town like my son, to fly da planes." Then his tone lightened. "But you bedder get back to da program, or you miss da secont half."

Brandon checked his watch, "Oh thank you, you're right. I'll have to run or I'll be late." He hesitated a moment. "But what about you? Don't you have to get back too?"

Recompense

The man waved Brandon on with a laugh. "Yah, Yudas still hass much betraying und repenting to do, und hanging uf himself. But it takes a vhile to get to dat part. Besites, by now I know da qvickest vay back to da teater, so I make it fine. But you bedder run along so you don't miss nudding."

Taking his package, Brandon hastened from the shop, calling back, "It was nice talking to you again!" Then he hesitated. Why did I say "again", he wondered? Why? He really didn't understand.

Brandon hurried back toward the theater, his mind still mulling his exchange with the shopkeeper. As he moved along, he glanced inside the bag he was carrying to check his purchase. He noticed a business card which the man at the shop had included with the figurine. Taking out the card as he walked rapidly on, Brandon saw the name of the individual with whom he had been speaking. He came to an abrupt halt, overwhelmed by a feeling of confusion mingled with apprehension. The name he saw was "Johann Schisler."

For a moment, Brandon stood still, completely mystified. What was significant about that name? Why did it have such an impact on him? And why did it somehow sound so familiar?

Then he remembered. His sense of anxiety deepened as he muttered out loud, "Schisler! My God, wasn't that the name of the man who first brought the Black Plague into Oberammergau?"

Chapter X

Brandon eased quietly into his seat, just as the heralds on stage announced the beginning of the second half of the Passion Play. Margaret turned from her place in front of him to whisper, "Are you feeling better?"

Brandon smiled and nodded, mouthing "Thank you" in return. Then he settled back to enjoy the musical introduction by the chorus and to observe the evolving spectacle before him. So far, so good, he thought. Maybe he'd be luckier this afternoon than he had been at the morning's production.

It was not to be. As the presentation progressed to portray the agonies of Christ's trial and conviction, Brandon was again propelled precipitously into an agony of his own. This time, the headache pain set a whole new zenith of anguish. The throbbing, explosive pressure was unlike anything he had ever experienced before. Its intensity made him fight to avoid crying out, pleading for something, anything, to relieve the excruciating misery. He clenched his fists, pressed his eyes tightly shut, bit his lip, his entire body stiffening against the torture. Nothing helped.

Reverting to the only avenue of escape he had been able to devise, Brandon sank back and began the retreat into his own private mental world. By force of will, by compelled avoidance, he began to shut out the pain as he drifted ever deeper into reverie, away from the suffering.

Recompense

Descending farther and farther into a subconscious state, he felt relief gradually emanating from unreality.

As the haze enshrouding his mind slowly lightened and lifted, Brandon gazed around in surprise. He found himself once more in the same mysterious mountain village he had encountered earlier on the airplane. It was all still as it had been~the winding street, the Alpine houses, the flowers, even the distinctive mountain peak standing guard in the background. But this time he realized with a start that he knew *exactly* where he was. He was in Oberammergau! That mountain was the Kofelberg! There could be no mistaking the flavor of the town, even though it was much smaller and more bucolic, as though untold years of change had been stripped away.

Most significant of all, now the hamlet was not deserted. Rather, it was inhabited by real villagers~talking, laughing, working, busily going about their daily activities as they must have done for centuries. A genial spirit of well-being seemed to pervade the whole.

Brandon saw a boy ambling casually down the street, peering into shop windows as he went by, waving to an occasional acquaintance. The boy was about twelve years old, with a slight build, dark curly hair, and bright blue inquisitive eyes.

Something seared indelibly into Brandon's consciousness as he watched: instinctively, irrefutably he knew that, somehow, *he* was that boy! He was observing *himself* in another time, another era! He felt himself detached and yet totally aware. Could such a transformation be possible? He didn't know. All that was certain in his mind was that he *knew* he was experiencing such a phenomenon, whether he could explain it or not.

The boy stopped in front of a neatly-decorated building whose sign, in its wrought-iron frame, protruded into the street proclaiming "Scheerer's Bake Shop." For a time he inspected the offering of goodies displayed in the shop window. Then he went inside.

"Why, good day, Rolf," the middle-aged, pleasant-faced proprietress greeted him cheerily. "Are you here for your usual morning cookie? I just got some out of the oven." The discourse was naturally in German, which, to Brandon's surprise, he understood perfectly.

The delightful aroma of fresh-baked cookies permeated the shop. It seemed to have become a perpetual component of the good-humored owner, as well, following her wherever she went. She smiled broadly at young Rolf, wiping her hands on her apron and placing them on her ample hips.

"Hello, Mrs. Scheerer," Rolf responded politely. "Yes, I think I'd like a sugar cookie today, please."

Once he had indicated his preference, the boy's eyes swept quickly around the shop, as though searching for someone. A look of disappointment crossed his face, and his attention returned to Mrs. Scheerer.

"Good choice. I'm sure you'll enjoy it," she was saying, holding a tray from which Rolf could choose. He made his selection carefully, with earnest deliberation, trying not to be too obvious about picking one of the larger ones.

"Thank you. It smells delicious." Rolf handed Mrs. Scheerer the customary coin.

She placed the tray on the counter as the boy turned to leave, then called out in mock dismay: "My goodness, Rolf, here's a broken one. You'd better take it, too. I'll never be able to sell this one."

She handed Rolf the broken cookie, one he had failed to notice in his careful inspection, and smiled happily at the pleasure in the boy's eyes.

"Thank you again, Mrs. Scheerer." As he left the shop, he called back, "I'll see you tomorrow."

Mrs. Scheerer again wiped her hands on her apron, obviously pleased with herself, and returned to her baking.

Rolf continued down the street, munching the tasty morsels as he went. He had no place he had to be today, so he could take advantage of one of the last carefree days of summer before the fall school term began. It was a day meant to be enjoyed to the fullest~a bright blue sky overhead enhanced by a few wispy clouds, a warm autumn sun, the smells of late summer's harvest season everywhere.

He paused for a minute to admire the intricate murals covering the exterior of the Hotel Alte Post as he passed. It was one of the newer buildings in town. Rolf's mother had told him about the excitement surrounding opening of the hotel when she was a young girl in the village. It had been designed to offer accommodations for traders passing through the area with their wares, and so had also served as a contact for the isolated hamlet to receive information from the outside world.

Arriving next at the blacksmith shop, set well back from the street, Rolf meandered in to watch the stocky, vigorous artisan rehearse his craft. The boy was fascinated by the sparks, the glowing embers of the forge, the hammered staccato of creativity. He stood silently but observing closely, trying not to interrupt the rhythmic beat of the hammer shaping crude metal into a work of art, as the blacksmith fashioned part of an intricate wrought-iron gate.

"Ach, goot morning, Rolf," the smith greeted him, putting down his hammer when he spotted the boy. "You're here for your daily lesson in blacksmithing, yah?" He laughed heartily at his own effort at humor.

"Good morning, Herman. No, I'm just here to watch." He extended an offering toward the craftsman. "Would you like half of my cookie?"

"Ach, thank you, my boy," Herman said, accepting the donation and patting the boy affectionately on the shoulder. "You're a goot boy." He held up the nearly completed gate for Rolf to see. "You like what I make?"

"It's beautiful, Herman," the boy responded enthusiastically. "I wish we had one just like that at our house."

Herman smiled broadly, clearly very pleased by Rolf's praise. "Ach, it's not so much. You can make one for yourself when you become a blacksmith."

Rolf laughed, shaking his head. "No, I'll just buy one from you when I save up enough money."

"Oh, ho! That sounds like you might not be planning to become my apprentice after all. I was hoping you were about ready to start training for your life's work. Blacksmithing is hard, but it makes a goot living. You could learn a lot in my shop."

"Thank you, Herman. I know I'd really like working with you. But I want to stay in school a little longer. I really like books, and reading, and learning about new places and ideas." Rolf paused briefly, then continued, "I know it's not a job or anything, but that's what I like."

Herman slapped the boy approvingly on the back. "Ach, that's goot, Rolf. You do that. You stay in school. You enjoy those books. There'll always be old men like me to do the other kinds of work." He chuckled as he looked dotingly at the boy. "Some people work with their hands, some people work with their heads. You're a smart boy, Rolf. You go and use your head. Leave the gate-building to old men like me." Again, he broke into a hearty laugh at his own witticism.

Rolf smiled and turned to leave the shop. "I'd better let you get back to work now. Otherwise, you'll never get your gate finished."

"Come see me again soon," Herman called after him. Rolf heard the measured cadence of the hammering resume behind him as he headed down the street.

Continuing his stroll, Rolf wandered past tidy, well-kept homes, their yards and gardens enlivened by a colorful profusion of flowers. In the background could be seen the ever-present mountains, dominated by the Kofelberg, a comforting, enveloping presence. Rolf stopped and drew in a deep breath of appreciation.

At the end of the street, outlined against the blue sky, rose the distinctive spire of the village church. To Rolf, it was a familiar, reassuring sight. For as long as he could remember, he had attended services at that church regularly with his mother. She had found solace and serenity there, particularly after the death of her husband, Rolf's father, less than a year after the boy's birth.

While working at his job as woodsman in the nearby Alpine forests, she had told Rolf, his father had been badly crushed by a tree carelessly felled by a fellow woodsman. Shortly after the accident, he had died, leaving the young widow to raise their son alone, supporting them both as best she could through her skills as a seamstress.

Under these trying circumstances, support from kindly neighbors and an understanding parish priest had been crucial. Thus, Rolf's mother had become ever more closely associated with her church, and young Rolf had come to accept the conjuncture as a normal facet of his life.

Now, as Rolf approached the place of worship, he saw the priest busily tending flowers in the churchyard~clipping a bit here, trimming there, stooping occasionally to pull a stray weed. Rolf stood at the gate for a time observing quietly before the cleric looked up from his task.

"Well, good morning, Rolf. Nice to see you," he greeted the youth genially. "I don't suppose you're here looking for a gardening job, are you?" he added with a chuckle.

"Good morning, Father. I'd be glad to help, if there's something I can do."

"There certainly is," the priest assured him, indicating several containers nearby. "Could you take those clippings to the trash pile out in back, please? Then bring the buckets back for the next load."

"Sure! I'll be right back," Rolf said as he set about his errand. He liked the personable parish priest and gained real satisfaction from feeling helpful.

The two worked side by side for a time, chatting companionably about village events. During a brief lull, Rolf determined to pose a more serious topic of conversation, something he had long wondered about.

"Father, do you believe that God gives us rewards when we're good and punishes us if we're bad?"

The priest looked closely at the boy, surprised by this sudden shift in the dialogue.

"Hmmm, that's a difficult question, Rolf. Why do you ask? Is there a problem?"

"No, not really. It's just that people always seem to thank God when bad things don't happen to *them*. They say God protected them. They don't seem to worry much when bad things happen to someone else, though. Maybe they think those people *deserve* to be hurt because they've done something bad."

The priest smiled, impressed by the seriousness with which the youth presented the issue. And he wasn't certain he had a logical answer.

"Well, Rolf," he began, "the Bible says 'God works in mysterious ways,' so maybe we can't figure out why things happen as they do. Do *you* think God never lets bad things happen to good people, only to bad people?"

Rolf pondered the question for a long moment, then answered slowly, "No, not really, Father, because some of my friends get sick or get hurt sometimes, and still they're really good." He paused again, then confessed, "And sometimes I kind of wish that bad things really would happen to some of the people who are mean~but they don't. Bad people just seem to get away with things at times and not get punished. So I don't understand how it all works."

The priest patted Rolf on the shoulder. "You've given this lots of thought, I can tell. I wish I had a simple answer for you, but I don't think there is one. Have you considered this: maybe God doesn't either reward us *or* punish us for being good or bad. Maybe God's plan is for things to just happen naturally, and then see how we respond. Maybe the *real* test is to see how we handle both good things and bad things when they happen to us. Could that be, Rolf?"

The boy contemplated the concept seriously before replying. "You might be right, Father. I hope so." Then he asked quietly, "Would that mean that my father wasn't a bad person because he was killed?"

Recompense

"Oh, my, Rolf! Of course your father wasn't a bad person!" The priest put his arm around the youth's shoulders, trying to reassure him as best he could. "Your father was one of the kindest men I've ever known. Never forget that, Rolf. He may not have attended church services as often as I'd have liked, but he was a truly good person. He was fair, honest, loving, hard-working, all of the things a father should be. His death was an accident, not some sort of punishment. Can you believe that, Rolf?"

"Yes, Father, I think I can." Rolf's eyes glistened and his face radiated with relieved joy. "Thank you very much for telling me that." His smile of gratification continued to glow as he added, "I'd better be getting on now. But I'll be back. Thank you again."

"Thank *you*, Rolf. Come by anytime."

The priest watched with a sense of contentment as the boy headed down the street, softly whistling a favorite hymn.

CHAPTER XI

Deep in his trance, Brandon continued to witness the march of events in historic Old Oberammergau. It was proving to be both a mystifying and a fascinating experience.

As inconceivable as it seemed, he still saw *himself* as young Rolf on his inquisitive venture down the main street of the town. Rolf was absorbed in making the most of the splendid autumn day, enjoying his freedom from responsibilities as well as his personal contacts with the townspeople. Obviously well liked by his many acquaintances in the village, the boy responded warmly to their positive overtures.

Rolf's curiosity added to his relaxed pace. There were so many sights, so many distractions to entice a twelve-year-old, and he did his best to yield to all of them. A songbird voicing its happiness, a brightly colored flower, a bustling ant, a friendly puppy~all distracted him in turn and were rewarded with his momentary attention.

Approaching the impressive woodcarving establishment near the center of town, Rolf halted as he noticed some of his less-likable acquaintances emerge from the shop. They were the Grossveldt family~father, mother, a daughter Rolf's age, and a younger brother. Try as he might, Rolf had never been able to establish his customary easy-going relationship with them.

The father and mother were friendly in a distant way but always maintained an aloofness, seemingly based on their perceived superiority as "leaders" of the hamlet's business community. Mr. Grossveldt owned and operated the local slaughterhouse and prided himself in the financial success that had come from supplying meat to the surrounding communities. For Mrs. Grossveldt, ample finances were equated with social prominence, a position that she assumed and exercised with relish.

It was the children who had always been most difficult for Rolf to deal with. The daughter, Ursula, had evidenced for years an affection for Rolf, which he in no way reciprocated either by word or action. He had always been polite, but had never been attracted to her despite her attentions. She was overweight, demanding, rude to those she considered "beneath her station", an unpleasant person who flaunted in as many ways as possible the family's monetary success. Why she was infatuated with someone like Rolf with his limited resources he could never understand.

Even worse was the younger brother, Heinrich. Thoroughly spoiled by his doting parents, also overweight, he had learned at an early age that he could get almost anything he wanted if he whined, fussed, or clamored long enough. The adults appeared to be completely intimidated by him, finding it easier to acquiesce to his demands than to attempt even a modicum of discipline. As a rule, Rolf tried to avoid all contact with the disagreeable child.

Now, as the family came down the steps of the shop, young Heinrich was exhibiting his customary behavior. "I said I wanted the biggest wooden soldier," he whined. "Why did you have to buy me this little one? I want the big one."

"That will do, Heinrich," his mother admonished, almost mechanically. "Just be quiet."

"I won't! I'm going back there and get that big soldier. Just wait, you'll see!"

Ursula saw Rolf waiting for them to continue on their way, and put on her most provocative manner. "Hello, Rolf," she cooed, smiling archly and waggling her eyelashes. "It's *so* nice to see you."

"Good morning, Ursula," Rolf returned her greeting, trying to be pleasant. "And good morning to you, Herr Grossveldt, Frau Grossveldt." He nodded to the adults, then turned to Heinrich: "Hello, Heinrich."

Heinrich made a face and stuck out his tongue, sassing, "I don't have to talk to you."

"Heinrich, where are your manners?" his mother admonished. "Good morning, Rolf. I'm afraid our Heinrich is a bit out of sorts today."

"That's all right, Frau Grossfeldt. Pretty day, isn't it?"

"It certainly is. But we must be on our way. We must do more shopping for Ursula's new school things. We always like her to have every thing she needs." Mrs. Groosveldt gave her daughter an indulgent nudge.

"Goodbye, Rolf. See you at school soon," Ursula put in, smiling as flirtatiously as she could.

" 'Bye, Ursula. Good luck shopping." Rolf again nodded politely to the Grossveldts.

As he went up the steps of the wood-carver's shop, he heard Heinrich resume his protests: "I don't want to go looking for stupid school stuff for Ursula. Yuck! I want to go get my big wooden soldier. I want my soldier!" Fortunately, the shop door closed behind Rolf, shutting out Heinrich's petulant demands.

Looking around at the assortment of carved wooden items displayed on the shop's numerous shelves was always one of Rolf's favorite pastimes. His eyes moved slowly from piece to piece, appreciative of the skill and effort required to fashion them. At times he had tried a bit of woodcarving himself, with limited success, and for that reason the intricacy of the work before him impressed the youth even more.

Behind the counter, waiting on two customers who had evidently made a selection, was the shop's proprietor, Mr. Schisler. He was a large man, fully bearded, somewhat rotund. But those large hands had the delicate touch of genius when it came to woodcarving. Rolf had watched him on many occasions, by the hour, skillfully crafting his life-like items in the work area at the rear of the shop. Particularly beautiful were his statuettes of the Madonna and Child. Mr. Schisler was a more somber, less gregarious man than Herman, but he was nevertheless at least the equal of the blacksmith in artistry within his chosen medium.

The customers at the counter, their carefully packaged purchase in hand, turned to leave, and Rolf paused, surprised and delighted.

"Why, good morning, Fraulein Waldung. Hello, Inga. It's so nice to see you both."

"Hello, Rolf," Fraulein Waldung responded. "Are you enjoying your last days before school starts? Remember, I expect to see you in class next week, ready to put in a good year's work."

She was a tall, thin woman, not particularly pretty but neatly dressed in her somewhat severe attire. Her hair was fashioned in a large bun at the back of her head, which added to her image as the archetypal schoolteacher. Yet Rolf had always enjoyed being in her classroom, where she brooked no nonsense, maintaining both strict discipline and high standards of learning.

In turn, Rolf had the feeling that he was one of Fraulein Waldung's favorite students, along with Inga. Of course to Rolf, Inga was eminently a favorite in *every* way. She was the daughter of Mrs. Scheerer from the bakery shop, and had much the same cheerful, optimistic outlook on life. Her attractiveness stemmed from more than her exceptional youthful beauty. There was an irrepressible spirit about her, an exuberant buoyancy, that made her delightful company in any situation, and Rolf had long ago fallen under her spell. He tried to maintain a reserved, detached comportment, but with Inga that was impossible. He was bewitched.

Today she looked especially captivating. She was wearing a soft green Bavarian-style jumper over a crisp white blouse, with green ribbon lacing criss-crossed down the front. Her hair was also in traditional Bavarian braids, with dainty green ribbons bouncing at the ends. But it was the lithe, free, fluidity of her movement, perfectly natural and unaffected, along with her easy, airy laugh, that most impressed the boy of twelve. She might be a pal, an adventurous companion, but he could never forget that Inga was also a girl.

Now she stood quietly, smiling, waiting for Rolf to respond to Fraulein Waldung's dictum.

"Oh yes, sure, of course I'll be back in school," Rolf stammered. He found both women somewhat intimidating.

"Good!" declared Fraulein Waldung. "I was afraid you might be planning to do something foolish, like going to work at a regular job."

"Oh no, I'll be in school again," Rolf assured her, still a bit nervous. "I really like school and learning," he added lamely.

Inga gave him her brightest smile. "Then I'll be seeing you next week too, Rolf."

Rolf's eyes lit with pleasure. He desperately wanted to continue the conversation, so he addressed Inga: "I looked for you at the bakery this morning, but you weren't there. Maybe I'll see you tomorrow."

"That would be nice," Inga commented, favoring him with another of her radiant smiles. "I'll be looking for you. 'Bye, Rolf."

"Goodbye, Inga. Goodbye, Fraulein Waldung," Rolf replied, still somewhat flustered. He felt his face warm and redden, but the women were gone before they could notice.

Rolf breathed deeply and turned to watch Mr. Schisler, whose eyes held a knowing, slightly bemused look. The proprietor had witnessed the youth's discomfiture, and tried to put him at ease. "That Inga is a nice girl, isn't she?" he asked with a twinkle in his eye. "Did you know that she sometimes helps my son Kaspar's wife with their little ones, since Kaspar has been away?"

"No, I didn't," Rolf answered, anxious to change the subject. "Where did your son go?"

Recompense

"Oh, he found a job over in Eschenlohe for the summer. He couldn't find work here, he said, and he's not very good at woodcarving. So he decided to take a job helping with the harvest over there."

Mr. Schisler's nimble hands never slackened as he talked. Tiny slivers of wood escaped from his knife, falling like so many gentle raindrops. "But Kaspar does get lonesome for that little family of his," he continued. "I'm not sure how much longer he'll be able to stay away from them."

"Maybe he'll have enough money soon so he can come home," Rolf suggested. "Anyway, I'm glad Inga has been able to help with the children. I hope she won't be too busy to help out when school starts."

Neither infringed upon the ensuing silence for some time as the delicate face of a Madonna gradually emerged from its imprisoning wood. Rolf watched intently, fascinated, while Mr. Schisler's eyes reflected increasing satisfaction with his creation.

"I guess I'd better be going now," Rolf broke in softly at last. "Do you think it will be finished by tomorrow?"

"I believe so, Rolf. Why don't you stop by and check?" Mr. Schisler invited, as he continued shaping the wood.

"Thank you, I will. Goodbye now," Rolf said, leaving as quietly as he could, as though exiting a place of special reverence.

Outside, he encountered a profoundly contrasting scene. His attention was drawn instantly to a gathering locus of activity singularly unusual in his peaceful town. From every home and establishment, it seemed, people were pouring out to join a surging crowd of citizens hastily assembling in the Town Square. Some were running, some only quickening their steps, but no one was ignoring the flurry. Rolf looked on for a moment, amazed by the swelling bustle, before his own curiosity led him to join the converging throng. Everywhere there were anxious inquiries: "What's happening? What's going on?"

Reaching the square, Rolf utilized his slight size to worm his way toward the center of the assemblage. There, surrounded by shouting, posturing villagers, was an itinerate peddler, his pack clutched firmly before him, trying vainly to answer all of their questions at once. The situation had degenerated into utter pandemonium.

Suddenly, above the commotion, rose an authoritative voice demanding, "What's going on here? What's the meaning of all this?" The deep, stentorian tones commanded instant respect. Frenzied bedlam halted, and a hushed lull came over the crowd as they turned to view the familiar figure of their revered Burgermeister descending the steps of the Town Hall.

"I said, what is going on here?" he demanded a second time. "Have you all gone mad?"

A villager standing behind the peddler summoned sufficient courage to push the besieged vendor forward. "It's this man's fault. He's come here telling wild stories, frightening everyone."

The Burgermeister stepped directly in front of the trembling peddler, drawing himself up in his most magisterial manner. "So! You're the one!" he stated in clear, accusatory tones. "What do you have to say for yourself? Speak up, man. Why have you disturbed our peaceful village?"

The peddler looked around fearfully, seeming to realize that he would receive no sympathy from this mob.

"Speak up, man!" the Burgermeister repeated.

The visitor faced the Burgermeister and proceeded in a quavering voice: "I'm terribly sorry, Herr Burgermeister, to bring your townspeople bad news. I didn't mean to cause all this trouble. It's just that I felt I must warn you good folk."

"Warn us about what?" the Burgermeister maintained his stern, inquisitorial demeanor. "What are you doing here? Where do you come from?"

"Please, sire, I've been trying to tell your people. I'm just a poor peddler, trying to sell my wares. Let me leave, and I won't bother you anymore. I only thought you would want to know what's happening out there." His eyes pleaded for understanding.

"What are you talking about?" the Burgermeister queried sharply. "What could possibly be happening that would give you the right to come into our peaceful town and create such hysteria? For heaven's sake, man, speak up!"

Seeing that the official was finally ready to hear him out, the vendor spoke more boldly: "You see, sire, I've been traveling around the country, and everywhere I go I hear the same story. I've been avoiding all of the villages in case it's true, but it seemed safe here, so I came in to pick up a supply of food."

"You still haven't answered my question. You're not making any sense," the Burgermeister insisted angrily, as the crowd grumbled. "What's happening out there?"

"It's the plague, sire. The plague! People are dying by the thousands! They're stacking them in the *streets*!"

"What did you say?" questioned the Burgermeister, suddenly ashen faced, his tone a mixture of fear and incredulity.

"The *plague*! It's back! It's spreading all over the land. They're calling it the 'Black Death'!"

Chapter XII

Within minutes of the peddler's momentous announcement, the townspeople of Oberammergau gave way to sheer panic. Despite the best efforts of the Burgermeister to restore a sense of order, citizens surrendered to their deepest fears, and the result became a village in chaos.

Some stood shrieking, crying out at the invisible terror, as though trying to restrain it through the volume of their protests. Others headed for the church at the end of the street~at first in an orderly, purposeful manner, then in a wild uncontrolled rush~to plead for Divine intervention. One man proclaimed loudly from the steps of the Town Hall, "Woe is us! We are all doomed! It is the just judgement of a wrathful, angry God." No one seemed inclined to stop, to think, to settle on a reasonable course of action.

Rolf found himself in the vortex of the turmoil, buffeted by the surging movement around him. He stayed near the Burgermeister, hoping that such a respected individual might still the tumult, but it was hopeless. Rolf could only wonder how people kept from being trampled or crushed in the melee.

Gradually, as the unruly crowd streamed from the Square, some of the calmer citizens were able to begin discussing how best to meet their very real crisis. Everyone seemed to recognize the gravity of the situation. There had been previous outbreaks of the plague, and no one dared to underestimate its potential for devastation. Even though the last epidemic had occurred many years earlier, the villagers still talked in hushed tones about its horrors~for those who had been infected with the insidious malady, as well as its aftermath for the stricken communities.

Thus, Rolf had come to learn and to fear the gruesome symptoms that would signal an outbreak of the disease. First, the individual would come down with a high fever, accompanied by chills, headache, vomiting, and sometimes by complete delirium. The true harbinger, however, would be large, painful swellings or lumps in the armpit, neck, or in the groin area. These protuberances might grow, filling with festered matter, until they actually burst. Sometimes the hemorrhages would contain dried blood, black in color, leading to the label "Black Death". And once the impurities contaminated the blood, or spread to the lungs, which was often the case, death would follow in a matter of days.

Now, all of these doleful tales of misery which had been recounted in whispers over the years suddenly became very real. Perhaps what had always concerned Rolf most as stories of past contagion were told and retold was that no one seemed to know its *cause*. He knew there was little chance of survival once one became contaminated, but he had always hoped that somehow, someone might devise a means of protecting the populace against its ravishes. So far, he knew, no one had been able to do so.

A sudden thought struck the youth: When I grow up, maybe that will be *my* job. If I work really hard and study everything, maybe I can find the *cause* of this "Black Death" so people won't have to die from it anymore. It was a mission to ponder, both exhilarating and daunting.

Those few individuals who had not yet succumbed to the general hysteria gathered around the Burgermeister~somber, apprehensive, but determined to find the best path to pursue. After exchanging ideas for a time, the Burgermeister finally recommended that they all go home to look after their families. "We can't act in haste," he cautioned. "We would only make matters worse." That evening, when they had all had more time to evaluate the situation, he promised he would call into session the full Council of the Six and Twelve, the hamlet's governing body comprised of both civic and religious leaders. Perhaps then some workable decisions could be made.

Throughout the long afternoon, tensions heightened as the villagers remained trapped in the gloom of their own despair. Everywhere, melancholy observations or dire predictions reflected the hopelessness that had infected the populace as powerfully as the anticipated plague. There was only one place that Rolf could find which had not given in to the general despondency, and that was Mrs. Scheerer's Bake Shop.

"Come in, Rolf, have a cookie," invited the genial proprietress when the youth wandered over to her shop. "We have to keep going about our daily lives, so we may as well make the best of it."

"Why is everyone so afraid, Mrs. Scheerer? Are we all going to die?"

"No, no, no, Rolf! Don't even think such a thing. People become afraid when they don't understand things, that's all."

"But even the Burgermeister doesn't know what to do."

"He'll think of something, don't you worry. When the Council meets tonight, they'll come up with a plan that will work. Our town will be all right," Mrs. Scheerer stated in her reassuring way.

Rolf felt better, and tried to smile as he nibbled his cookie. With new confidence, he looked around the shop. "Is Inga here, Mrs. Scheerer?"

"I'm sorry Rolf, she isn't. She's gone over to the Schislers again to help with the children. Mrs. Schisler was especially concerned for her little ones."

Disappointed, Rolf turned to leave. "Thank you for the cookie, Mrs. Scheerer, and thanks for what you said. I'm sure you're right. Maybe everything will be all right after all." But his eyes still held a doubt.

"You're most welcome, Rolf. I'll tell Inga you were looking for her."

When the boy reached his small home, set amidst an assortment of trees and flowers on a quiet street beyond the Town Square, his anxious mother greeted him with both relief and joy.

Recompense

"Oh Rolf, I'm so happy you're back. I was worried about you being gone for so long," she declared, giving him a warm hug. She was a small woman~Rolf was almost her equal in height~with a pretty face, its delicate lines reflecting cultured refinement. Her light brown hair was neatly arranged, and the clothes she had sewed for herself indicated both style and good taste. But the most distinctive feature about her perhaps was her eyes. They were large, dark brown in color as opposed to the bright blue hue the son had inherited from his father, and they mirrored an intense vitality that seemed to draw people to her automatically. Her ready smile, like that of Rolf, added to her image as a loving, caring human being.

"Hello, Mama," the youth responded happily, returning her embrace and reverting to his childhood name for her in the stress of the day. "I didn't mean to worry you. It's just that there was so much excitement everywhere that I forgot the time."

"Yes, yes, I understand. The whole village seems to have temporarily lost its senses." She looked closely at her son, deep concern in those expressive eyes. "Are you sure you're all right?"

"Oh yes, Mother, I'm fine. You're right about the town, though. No one seems to know what to do." Then he added hopefully, "But Mrs. Scheerer says everything will be all right. She thinks the Council of the Six and Twelve will come up with a plan."

Rolf's mother tried to sustain his optimism. "I'm sure Mrs. Scheerer is right. She's very perceptive. We'll just have to wait and see what happens." Then she added, as an afterthought, "I do hope the Council is less emotional about things than the people were at the church. I went there to pray when I heard the terrible news, and the poor Father was having an awful time trying to calm everyone. Some even thought we should hang the peddler for bringing our town such bad news, but Father finally got them all settled down."

"Can we go to the Council meeting tonight and see what they decide?" Rolf asked, pleading in his voice.

"Yes, I think we should. I'm sure the whole village will be there. But now you'd better have something to eat."

She brought him a bowl of hearty vegetable soup that she had kept warm, along with a wedge of cheese and some bread and butter. Rolf devoured them as appreciatively as only a hungry twelve-year old boy can do. Mother and son then passed the remaining interval in pleasant, personal conversation until time for the evening meeting.

Anticipation mingled with apprehension characterized the gathering of the citizens of Oberammergau. Panic had been temporarily tempered by faith in the ability of the village leaders to ascertain some solution to the impending crisis. An air of anxious expectancy buoyed the spirits of those who had earlier given way to utter despair.

Council members took their places at the long raised table, while villagers settled into the rows of chairs or stood crowded along the walls of the Town Hall. With the Burgermeister wielding his gavel, the meeting was called to order.

"We all understand the gravity of the situation that has brought us here tonight," the Burgermeister began. "Above all, we must avoid a repetition of the hysteria we saw earlier today. If we keep our heads, we can perhaps solve the problem. If we give in to fear, we become helpless."

He looked around at his fellow townspeople, encouraged by their nods of assent. Taking a deep breath, he went on. "Now then, we've all had time to think about the dilemma our village faces. Let me assure you, it is not to be taken lightly. We know the consequences of inaction. So I propose that each Council member tell us what he feels we should do to resolve our problem. After discussion, we'll settle on a unified course of action."

A general murmur ran through the assembled crowd, with whispers and vigorous head-nodding signaling agreement. "So, who would like to speak first?" the Burgermeister invited, looking around at his Council members.

The members exchanged glances, each waiting for his counterpart to set forth the first suggestion.

"Come, come, gentlemen," urged the Burgermeister. "This is no time to be hesitant."

The Council member at the end of the table cleared his throat and made his tentative proposal: "I've heard that the plague is carried in the air by vapors. Sometimes you can smell them, sometimes you can't. I'm told that the best thing to do is to build a huge fire at each entrance to the town. The fires will draw the vapors away and carry them upward in the smoke, where they can do no harm."

"It would be nice to find so simple a solution," the Burgermeister noted. "It couldn't hurt to try. What do the rest of you think? How about you, Herr Grossveldt?"

"You want my opinion?" asked the slaughterhouse owner rhetorically. "I'll tell you what I think. Until we get rid of the real cause of all this evil, we can build as many fires as there are in hell and it won't help." His tone was that of one who has the absolute truth, with no possibility of error or contradiction.

"What do you mean, Herr Grossveldt?" one of the other Council members inquired. "What is this 'real cause' that you speak of?"

Mr. Grossveldt turned to the speaker with a smug, condescending smile and responded as one enlightening a child: "Why, the Jews, of course!" His statement left no room for question. "Everyone knows that the Jews are unclean and dishonorable. They run from village to village with their wares, spreading their filth in pursuit of money. That's why we should have hanged that peddler before he could get away and do more damage. He was undoubtedly a Jew."

"Now, now, Herr Grossveldt, we cannot be too hasty," cautioned the Burgermeister. "There is no evidence that the plague is connected in any way with our Jewish neighbors…"

"Who needs evidence?" Grossveldt interrupted. "We all know the Jews are nothing but trouble. Why, did you know there's even a rumor that some Jew plans to build another slaughterhouse in the area, in competition with mine, forcing lower prices?" He looked around, certain that he had made an incontrovertible case.

There was a moment of embarrassed silence before another Council member spoke up. "Maybe we shouldn't be looking for someone else to blame," he suggested. "Maybe we should look more closely at *ourselves* to be sure this isn't some type of punishment from God, because of the sin in our midst."

"How can you even think such a thing?" Grossveldt objected. "It's obvious the Jews are to blame."

The Burgermeister held up his hand for order. "Let's hear him out. What is it you are suggesting?"

Noticeably intimidated by Grossveldt's opposition, the Council member nevertheless went on. "Perhaps we should call for a day of prayer to ask for God's forgiveness and deliverance. Or maybe we could build a special shrine to the saints. St. Roch of Montpelier has been said to have special powers to halt the plague. Maybe we should show our reverence to him, or maybe to the blessed Virgin." He looked at the audience, somewhat defensive but sincere in his manner.

"A day of prayer could certainly be beneficial," the Burgermeister concurred. "We'll add it to our list for consideration. Now, are there any other suggestions?"

Another Council member who had been silent so far took the opportunity to voice his thoughts. "I don't think any of the recommen-dations made so far can save our village. It will take much more drastic action, I'm afraid. That's why I think our only hope is to abandon our homes, our entire village, and move away into the hills until all of this danger passes. Perhaps then, when its safe once again, we can come back and try to start over."

The extremeness of his suggestion caught the villagers by surprise, but they were quick to pronounce their objections to so radical a measure. Cries of "No, never! We'll never leave our homes!" sounded through the Hall.

The Burgermeister rapped the table, struggling to restore decorum. "People! People! Let us have order! I can assure you that I personally oppose abandoning our beloved Oberammergau. But we must make our decision in a disciplined fashion. Please, no more outbursts."

Slowly, through a process of compromise and agreement, the Council of the Six and Twelve settled on a plan of action that incorporated several of the suggestions, with the exception of Mr. Grossveldt's, or abandonment of the village, which was ruled out. The Council finally settled on a type of "quarantine" instead: armed guards would be posted at all entrances to the town, and no one would be allowed to leave or come in from the outside. Hopefully, isolation from all other communities would ensure that the plague was not brought into their hamlet. Additionally, fires would be maintained at the entrances, as recommended, and a day of prayer to beseech God's mercy would be set.

"Herr Burgermeister," one of the men in the audience called out as the proceedings moved toward a close, "shouldn't we be posting those guards right away, tonight? We must not take any chances. I, for one, will volunteer to spend the night on guard, if you wish."

Voices of support rose from the assembled villagers: "Yes, I'll help too," "Count me in," "And me." Hands were raised to indicate a willingness to serve.

"Good, good. I knew I could count on you good people," the Burgermeister responded with satisfaction. "Volunteers, please meet with me after the meeting is adjourned. Now, the rest of you, please go get a good night's rest. The days ahead will require all of our energies."

Exhausted, but with new hope, the townspeople drifted from the meeting. Some headed for the local Bierkeller to review the dramatic events of the day over a brimming stein, while others, like Rolf and his mother, made their way to their homes with the expectation that tomorrow would be a better day.

CHAPTER XIII

The next day did dawn on a much brighter note. The actions taken by the Council of the Six and Twelve, the fact that there was an actual plan to put into operation, seemed to engender a new spirit of optimism among the residents of Oberammergau. Once again, there was reason for hope.

Adding to the sense of growing confidence was the fact that the Burgermeister had moved quickly to implement decisions made the night before. Already, armed guards could be seen stationed at their positions around the village, and the Burgermeister was even then instructing the next group who would serve in the relay to prevent any entrance or exit whatever, into or out of their hamlet.

Further, large fires were burning at the main entrances, their ascending smoke seeming to provide visual evidence that the deadly vapors were somehow being drawn away from the threatened populace. And finally, a time of special prayer had been scheduled for all of the following day, culminating in an evening service at the village church. With all of these procedures in place, hopefully everything would soon be well once more.

As the day wore on, the spark of encouragement continued to glow, inspiring a return to more normal activities on the part of the villagers. Of course, everywhere in town the major topic of conversation remained the plague, but now it was no longer assumed that there was no possibility of escape from its doom. Thanks to the timely actions of their Burgermeister and the Council, Oberammergau would be safe.

The change in mood was evident as Rolf made his lingering way down the village's main thoroughfare. At the Bake Shop, the comforting atmosphere of the previous day still pervaded, with Mrs. Scheerer's genial smile belying any threats to their little haven.

"It looks like you were right, Mrs. Scheerer," Rolf told her cheerfully. "Everything seems to be fine today, just like you said."

"I'm glad to hear that, Rolf. Of course, there could still be trouble, but it doesn't help a bit to give in to panic, does it?"

Rolf's attention turned to Inga, who looked her usual radiant self. "Isn't it good that things are settling down, so that school can start like always next week? Yesterday I was afraid nothing would ever get back to the way it should be."

Inga's luminous smile appeared to brighten the entire shop as she responded, "Yes, I'm really glad that good sense won out over all the fear. We have so much to be happy about here, don't we Rolf?" She paused, her expressive eyes now mirroring sincere concern. "Poor Mrs. Schisler, she was so frightened yesterday, all alone with those sweet children and her husband not there to help. I do hope he'll be able to come home soon, once there's no more need for the guards outside the town."

"That would be nice for all of them," Rolf agreed. "In the meantime, I'm sure you've been a big help to her, Inga."

Once more her effervescent smile lit the room. "Thank you, Rolf, it's kind of you to say that." Inga's eyes lowered for a moment, but the look of pleasure remained. To turn attention from herself, she added, "Don't forget your cookie."

Rolf made his careful selection, a brown-sugar cookie with nuts this time, handing Mrs. Scheerer his coin. "Thank you both. I'll see you tomorrow," he said, and headed down the street.

Recompense

The rest of the day was spent in pleasant idleness. Rolf missed seeing Herman, but the sign attached to the door of the blacksmith shop indicated that the smith was engaged elsewhere: "Closed: on Guard Duty", it read. Through the window, the young man glimpsed the now-completed wrought-iron gate, even more beautiful than he had imagined.

As the youth ambled on through town with no great purpose in mind, he suddenly stopped, remembering something. The Burgermeister had placed guards carefully at all of the town entrances, Rolf knew, but there was one further potential problem he had just thought of. Unknown to the adults of the community, but a well-kept secret among some of the older children, was the fact that there was another *hidden* means of entering or leaving their village. It was a small tunnel, part of an ancient aqueduct system, that burrowed under part of the town and emerged in a concealed alcove behind a heavy clump of woods nearby. The exit was completely secluded, due to the tangled underbrush that had overgrown the area. Inside the hamlet, the entrance was equally difficult to detect, since it could be reached only from a tree-shrouded root-cellar in the back yard of one of the homes nearby.

Within just the past year, Heinz, one of Rolf's friends, had discovered the tunnel. The boy had been clearing and enlarging their old cellar to hold an especially large crop of potatoes when he accidentally broke through the crumbling stone wall of the aqueduct. Unsure of what he had discovered, Heinz had boarded up the breach, leaving the prize to be explored later with the help of some of his more daring friends.

Rolf had been among that group, and the youngsters were thrilled by the significance of their find. Not only did it provide them with a camouflaged outlet, but after some of the old debris had been cleared and candles were acquired to provide light, the tunnel also served as an ideal covert hideaway where secret meetings could be held. The boys had whiled away countless, happy hours there, playing out their imaginative adventures and fantasies as knights, pirates, or brigands.

All had taken a solemn vow not to disclose their private treasure. However, Rolf had recently come to suspect that *someone* in the group had violated that sacred oath. Rumors and furtive whisperings hinted that one of the boys had surreptitiously taken a friend, one of the girls from the village, to the tunnel in an effort to impress her that he had not been idly boasting when he told her there was something very special he knew about. Who the young woman might be Rolf had no idea, but the disquieting feeling of betrayal remained nevertheless.

What concerned him now was that the tunnel could possibly provide a means of circumventing the quarantine instituted by the Burgermeister. Still, its existence was known to so few and the chances of its use to enter the town so remote that such a possibility seemed highly unlikely. Rolf determined that he would not risk dishonor by breaking his own vow of secrecy.

With his decision made, the youth went on about his usual activities. The remainder of the day passed with no new crises and with little to disturb his growing feelings of reassurance.

The following day had been designated as the day for special prayers, when villagers were to turn first to introspection, making sure that their thoughts or propensities were not such that they would bring retribution from Almighty God. Secondly, they were to entreat their Heavenly Father to spare their town from the ravages of the plague, if possible, and to give thanks to Him for His mercies so far. Only through Divine intervention, they were told, could their community be assured of survival.

Citizens of Oberammergau took the charge seriously, as they did all expressions of devout deportment. In private homes, many community members like Rolf and his mother set aside other obligations in order to devote time to sincere prayer and expressions of gratitude. Others gathered in small groups, or joined the ongoing procession to the church to make their pleas. Although some secular business was conducted as usual, primary effort was poured into what was considered the more pressing *sacred* business of invoking the blessing of a merciful God.

As evening approached, the stream of church-goers reached flood stage, with all townspeople seemingly eager to demonstrate their piety and devotion. The village priest had difficulty accommodating the huge crowd, but still made sure everyone felt welcome and appreciated. "It would be wonderful," he told them, "if this type of ecclesiastical outpouring could occur without the overshadowing threat of disaster. But whatever our motivation, be assured that God hears us and will give heed to our appeals."

While the villagers continued their earnest entreaties of faith, a small figure was moving slowly, stealthily through the shadows of the hamlet on a mission destined to impact their futures as no other event in the history of Oberammergau had done. That ominous individual was none other than young Heinrich Grossveldt. Through a combination of feigned illness and incessant fussing, he had convinced his parents to leave him home alone when they went to attend the community service that evening. Now, he set out to accomplish what he *really* had in mind.

Ever since the Burgermeister had instituted the quarantine, Heinrich had become increasingly frustrated and disgruntled. It wasn't that he particularly needed or even wanted to go anywhere outside the village. Rather, what galled him was being told that he *couldn't* do so. Always ready to insist on doing what he was told not to, Heinrich took the constraints of the quarantine personally, as if they had been designed purely to inhibit his freedom of movement. Therefore, he had stubbornly determined that, whatever the cost, he would find a way out of the town.

At first he had merely approached the guards at the entrances and demanded that they let him pass.

"You'd better let me go by here or you'll be in serious trouble," Alan had warned. "My Dad owns the slaughterhouse, and we've got lots of money, so if you don't let me through I'll tell my Dad and then you'll be sorry!"

But those worthy individuals, much as they might be intimidated by the elder Grossveldt's wealth and pretensions of superiority, were even more steadfast in their loyalty to their widely respected Burgermeister. Despite Heinrich's threats and tantrums, the guards had remained firm in maintaining Oberammergau's isolation.

The querulous youngster was not to be denied, however. In his anger, he recalled something that had occurred weeks before and which now might provide just the right avenue to evade the guards and have his way.

One evening, his sister Ursula had returned late from a stealthy rendezvous and was attempting to enter her room through an open lower window, undetected by their parents. Noiselessly, Heinrich had come up behind her.

"I see you, Ursula," he had announced in a hushed whisper. "You'd better tell me where you've been, or you're in big trouble."

"It's none of your business, you little brat!" Ursula retorted.

"It is too my business. If you don't say where you've been, I'm telling on you, so there!"

"You wouldn't dare!" challenged Ursula, her bravado beginning to fade. She knew only too well what Heinrich was capable of.

"Oh yeah, smarty? Just wait and see. If you don't tell me this minute, I'm going in and tell Mother and Father you've been sneaking around again. Then see what happens! How do you like that?"

Ursula realized from experience that the threat was genuine. Cornered, she relented. "Alright, you little brat. Who cares, anyway?"

With that, she told Heinrich briefly about the hidden tunnel that Heinz had showed her. Naturally, Heinrich insisted on seeing it too, *immediately*. After much arguing, Ursula convinced him to wait until the next day, since it would be difficult to find their way in the dark. So it was that Heinrich, still uttering his tattletale threats, had come to actually view the secret entrance that led to the exit from the village.

Recompense

Now he planned to utilize that information to evade the guards and achieve what he had so far been denied. To Heinrich, having his way was sufficient motivation to compensate for the effort involved.

"I'll show them," he muttered to himself as he moved cautiously but purposefully toward his goal. "They can't tell me what to do. Who does that Burgermeister think he is, anyway? He's probably one of those Jews. He can't make me stay in this dumb old town if I don't want to."

Young as he was, his perverse determination carried him on. With most of the villagers thoroughly occupied by their devotions at the church, the streets of Oberammergau were largely deserted, making it easy for the headstrong youngster to reach Heinz's house undetected. Once there, he slipped quietly through the back yard and down into the old root cellar. Pausing long enough to light the candle he had brought, Heinrich proceeded cautiously through the opening which Ursula had revealed under duress, and on into the forbidden tunnel.

A sense of elation gripped the youngster as he groped his way along the dark stone walls. He was going to make it! In spite of what the authorities had said, he was going to leave the village and return, without anyone knowing about it. "Just wait 'til Ursula finds out," he mumbled to himself, the prospect bringing a smile to his face. "That'll teach those guards to try to tell me I can't do something."

Faint moonlight showed through the tangle of overhanging brush at the tunnel's exit. Still smiling with self-congratulatory satisfaction, Heinrich parted the undergrowth and stepped out into the enclosed alcove. He gazed around, taking in a deep breath of triumph.

Without warning, Heinrich felt a firm hand clamp tightly over his mouth as strong arms gripped him from behind, lifting him from the ground. The candle dropped from his hand, sputtering out in the damp vegetation. Too startled and frightened to struggle at first, Heinrich now began thrashing about wildly, but to no avail. The arms restraining him held like bands of steel.

A voice whispered close to his ear, "Who are you? How did you get here?" Then, as the intruder seemed to realize that the boy could not respond in such a restraining grasp, the hands holding the youngster relaxed slightly while the hushed voice went on sternly, "I'm going to take my hand off your mouth now, but don't you dare make a sound. If you do, the guards will hear, and you know what that means, don't you?"

Gradually the suppressing hand relaxed. Heinrich, aware of the danger inherent in calling out, remained uncharacteristically silent, waiting for the interloper's next move. He felt himself being deposited back on the ground, released just enough so that he could turn to face his captor.

The wan moonlight provided scant illumination as it filtered through the overhanging branches of the encircling trees. But there was sufficient light, as the boy strained to see in the semi-darkness, for him to recognize the figure still deterring his movement. Regaining some of his customary bravado, Heinrich blurted out, "Why are you keeping hold of me? What do you think you're doing, anyway? I know who you are. You're Kaspar Schisler!"

Chapter XIV

"Ssshh! Be quiet! The guards will hear you." Kaspar Schisler warned, maintaining his grip on young Heinrich. "You're the Grossveldt boy, aren't you? How did you get here, anyway?"

"I don't have to tell you. You're not my boss," Heinrich retorted, back to his usual defiant self. "You're not supposed to be here. You know that no one from outside is allowed in town."

"Well then, what are *you* doing out *here*? You know that no one is allowed to *leave* Oberammergau either."

Heinrich had a ready answer: "They can't tell me what to do. I'm Heinrich Grossveldt, and my father owns the slaughterhouse. I can do whatever I want. So let go of me, right *now*!" The stubborn line of his chubby chin left no room for further argument.

"You still haven't told me how you got here, and I'm not letting go until you do," countered Kaspar. "I know you couldn't get past the guards, so what did you do?" His hold on Heinrich remained firm.

"Those guards aren't so smart. They don't even know about the secret tunnel," Heinrich boasted, eager to flaunt his successful evasion.

Kaspar was quick to see his opportunity. "What tunnel? What are you talking about?" He tightened his grip on the boy.

"Ow! You're hurting me! I told you to let go!"

"Shhh! Not until you tell me where that tunnel is."

"All right, all right! It's right over here. You don't have to be so mean," Heinrich whined. "Just let me go and I'll show you."

Cautiously, Kaspar released the boy, still vigilant for any attempt to escape or alert the guards. He was determined to find a means of entering the village and didn't want Heinrich to thwart his efforts now that he was so close.

Heinrich was still belligerent: "You sure waited long enough to let me go. Why are your hands so hot, anyway?

"Just tell me where the tunnel is!" Kaspar demanded, evading the question. He was not feeling well, and the boy was pushing his patience to the limit.

Once freed, Heinrich was ready to show off his knowledge of the hidden passageway. "It's right over here," he whispered, pointing through the undergrowth. "But first we have to find my candle I dropped when you grabbed me."

Groping about on hands and knees, they located the missing candle, but waited to re-light it until they had crawled through the tangled brush so the flicker of light would not give them away. Then, with Heinrich leading the way, the two carefully negotiated the underground corridor back to the root-cellar in Heinz's back yard.

As they got ready to go their separate ways, Kaspar once more grasped Heinrich firmly by both shoulders. "Thank you for showing me the tunnel," he told the boy, but added a warning: "Now, if you tell *anyone* that I'm back in town, remember that you broke the rules too, and you'll be in all kinds of trouble. Is that clear?"

Heinrich hesitated, torn between having to obey an order and his own self-preservation. He decided that his personal interests must come first. "All right, I won't, but you'd better not tell on me either, and I mean it!" With that, the two headed off in different directions.

Feeling steadily more ill, Kaspar determined to reach his small home on a side street of the village as quickly and quietly as possible. With the citizens of Oberammergau still engaged in their prayer service, he found it relatively simple to avoid detection.

Recompense

He neared his house with mounting excitement. It had been months since he had last seen his wife and children, and working far away from family and friends had led to almost unbearable loneliness. Even though he knew he was violating the town's well-intentioned quarantine, he felt that a brief, covert visit with his beloved family could do no harm. Then he would return to his job, with his clandestine homecoming undetected.

In the back of his mind, Kaspar admitted there was one further motivation for his journey home: the annual Kirchweih Fest was to be held that week-end. It was always a joyous three days of celebration throughout the region, commemorating the dedication of the local churches, and Oberammergau expected to join in with whole-hearted enthusiasm despite the limitations imposed by the quarantine. After a morning mass, the rest of the time would be given over to feasting, dancing, and general merry-making which Kaspar did not want to miss.

Cautiously, he approached the rear door of his little home and knocked lightly. There was no response. He knocked a second time, a bit more insistently, and was gratified to hear someone inside nearing the door.

"Who's there?" he heard his wife call out, her voice edged with tension.

"It's me…Kaspar," he answered, keeping his tone low, "Open up, Katrin. Please!"

A gasp of astonished recognition led to frantic rattling, as the latch was undone. The door swung wide, and with a cry of absolute joy, Kaspar's wife was enveloped in his arms.

"Kaspar, Kaspar, it's so good to have you home," she murmured in his ear, again and again. "I was so lonesome for you! I was afraid I might die and never see you again." She stepped back momentarily, surveying him as though he were an apparition. "But how did you get here? How did you get past the guards? Does anyone know you're here?"

"Not so fast, Katrin," Kaspar laughed, his arms again encircling his beloved. "Let me get the door closed first and I'll tell you. And where are our little ones? Are they all right?"

As if in answer to his query, a small, tousle-headed toddler appeared, sleepily rubbing his eyes with one fist and looking around uncertainly. "What is it, Mama?" he asked, not sure what had awakened him. Then he spotted Kaspar. Emitting a shriek of pure delight, he hurtled his small being pell-mell like a tiny missile toward Kaspar. "Papa! Papa! Papa! You're home!" he shouted in disbelief. "My Papa, I love you!"

Tears filled Kaspar's eyes as he held both his young son and his precious wife close. There was only one more element needed to make his joy complete. "Is my Marta asleep?" he inquired eagerly. "Can I see her, please?"

Still clutching her husband, as though fearful he might suddenly disappear, his wife led him to the small rocking-cradle in the corner of their cramped bedroom. By the flickering light of the candle Katrin held aloft, Kaspar looked down at the cherubic face of his baby daughter, innocently sleeping on through the clamor. With consummate tenderness, Kaspar leaned over to softly kiss her silken forehead. In his mind, the hazardous journey had all been made worthwhile.

Then he moved silently away from the cradle holding his priceless treasure and sank down on one of the wooden chairs in their sparse kitchen. It seemed as if the last of his diminishing energy had been drained away, and the enervating illness overwhelmed him. Little Johann clambered up on his lap, but Kaspar scarcely had strength left to hold him.

"Why Kaspar, what's wrong?" Katrin cried out, genuinely alarmed. In the excitement of her husband's unexpected return, she had failed to note the wan, taut look on his face or the feeble aspect of his bearing. Now it was inescapable. She held her hand to his forehead. "Oh Kaspar, you're ill!" she proclaimed. "You have a terrible fever. I must call the doctor at once!"

Recompense

"No, no, you can't," Kaspar protested. "Remember, I'm not supposed to be here. If anyone finds me, I could be arrested and taken to jail." He tried to smile, to reassure Katrin as best he could. "I'll be fine. I'm just tired from the trip over the mountains, that's all. If I rest a bit, I'll be all right."

She looked at her husband with deep concern in her eyes. "I hope you're right. We can't have anything happen now that we're together again. But what shall we do? We must get you well."

"I'll only be here for a few days, then I'll have to go back," Kaspar told her. "I don't think I better even take part in the Kirchweih, except here with you."

Katrin's eyes widened. "No, Kaspar, no! It must be just as it always was, with you here, like before." The protest in her voice echoed her longing.

He reached for her hand and pulled her close to himself and their young son. "I wish I could stay, more than anything. But I'll have to leave before anyone finds me. I'll just rest a while and get my strength back, and we'll enjoy our short time together." Looking lovingly into her eyes, he added, "Please don't be sad, Katrin."

Katrin brushed away a tear, responding as cheerfully as she was able, "You're probably right, Kaspar, dear. Let's just be together for now and worry about everything else when you're better again." With an affectionate smile, she picked up little Johann, telling him, "It's time you get back to bed, young man. Papa will still be here in the morning. Now he needs to get some sleep, too."

Gradually, peace and quiet returned to the Schisler household.

Unfortunately, Kaspar was not at all better the next morning. Added to the raging fever was a torturous headache that Katrin's loving attention and cold compresses could not alleviate. Increasingly concerned, she again insisted, "We'll *have* to call the doctor, Kaspar. Your fever isn't going down, not even a little bit. I'm really worried about you."

"Listen to me, Katrin, you know we can't do that. Do you want me to be arrested and locked up? I'm sure the fever will break soon. Please wait just a little longer."

Their exchange was interrupted by gentle knocking at the front door.

"Who could that be?" Kaspar whispered, alarm replacing the pain reflected in his eyes. "Have the authorities found out already?" He paused, remembering the night before. "If that little demon Heinrich…."

Katrin peered through the curtained window. "It's only Inga, come to help with the children. But we can't let her know you're here. I'll tell her I don't need help today. Just stay quiet."

Opening the door slightly, Katrin greeted the waiting young woman, "Good morning, Inga. It's nice to see you."

Before she could say more, Johann darted up behind her, peering around her skirts. On seeing Inga, he let out a whoop and headed directly to her. "Inga, Inga, my Papa comed home!" he squealed as she lifted him in her arms.

Inga looked at Katrin, surprised, not understanding.

"Oh, he just misses his Papa so," she said. "He'd like to think he's home with us."

"But he *is* home, Mama," Johann insisted. "Remember, he comed home last night. He's really home."

Katrin's face reddened. She took the child from Inga, stammering, "Don't pay any attention to him. He gets so excited." She recovered slightly. "Thank you for coming, but we won't need any extra help today, Inga. Maybe next week."

Inga flashed one of her enchanting smiles. "I'm glad you're doing well, Mrs. Schisler. I'll just help Mother in the shop today, instead. But I'm afraid I won't be able to come over next week, because school starts then and it will keep me pretty busy. So could I please say goodbye to the children before I go?"

Recompense

Not knowing how to refuse the innocent request, Katrin concurred. "Of course, Inga. Here's Johann. I'll bring Marta right out." She hoped the young woman would not think it strange that she was not invited into the home, as usual.

While Inga embraced Johann, telling him to be a good boy for his Mama, Katrin brought the gurgling Marta from the house. The baby cooed contentedly as Inga cradled her, displaying her own enticing smile.

"Your little ones are so dear, Katrin," Inga told her. "How lucky you are! I only hope their Papa can come home soon to see them, before they're all grown up."

Johann could contain himself no longer. "But Papa *is* home, Inga! He really is! He's in our house. Come and see, Inga," he insisted, tugging on her hand.

Immediately, Katrin intervened, "Now Johann, let Inga be on her way. You can see your Papa when he comes home." She snatched the boy up quickly in one arm, took the baby from Inga with the other, and hurried into the house.

Inga stood still for a moment, puzzled, looking at the house and wondering what was going on. Little Johann had seemed so *sure* that his father was home, and yet she knew the quarantine was being strictly enforced. And Katrin had appeared so uneasy, as though she were hiding something. It was all quite confusing. "Maybe Mother can help me make sense out of it," Inga thought as she walked back toward the Bake Shop.

Inside the Schisler home, meanwhile, events had reached crisis stage. Kaspar's fever continued to escalate, until at last he lapsed into delirium, alternately thrashing about on the bed or retreating into spasms of shivering. Nothing his wife could do, short of breaking her promise not to call in the doctor, could ease his suffering. It seemed almost merciful when he temporarily lost consciousness.

Toward evening, after the children had been fed and safely tucked into bed, the final blow fell. As Katrin was sponging off her husband, still desperately trying to reduce the fever, she noticed an ominous new development. On the side of Kaspar's neck, a lump had appeared, a type of swelling that appeared to grow even as she watched. A surge of panic swept over the distraught Katrin. Frantically, she raised his arm to inspect his armpit. Sure enough, another protuberance had materialized, this one even more pronounced, with tell-tale streaks of black and purple.

Katrin collapsed unto the bed beside her husband, unable to keep her nerveless body upright. Covering her face with her hands, she could only moan wretchedly, "Oh dear God, no, oh no," over and over, as she rocked back and forth. There could be no question as to what dreadful malady had struck her Kaspar. The signs were all too clear. And worst of all was the realization that there was absolutely nothing she could do now to safeguard her precious children.

CHAPTER XV

The following days were the most traumatic that Oberammergau would ever experience. Despite their carefully conceived plan to shield the community from the havoc of the pestilence decimating Europe, breaching of their security measures now left the village as vulnerable as all others. And in its march of death, the plague proved to be no respecter of persons.

First to suffer the terrors of its impact, the Schisler family also typified the plague's almost universal devastation. Kaspar lingered on through the succeeding day, but there was obviously no hope for his survival. His symptoms steadily worsened, until even light became intolerable, and the white coating on his tongue gradually thickened. Finally, his body could withstand the torturous agony no longer. Unknown to the other citizens of Oberammergau, the illness claimed its initial local victim.

By this time, Katrin and baby Marta were exhibiting early symptoms of the dread disease as well. Surprisingly, little Johann remained physically unaffected, though the bewildered youngster cried in despair when his Papa wasn't able to play with him. Despite her rising temperature and the throes of headache pain, despite her anguished grief, the despairing widow made her way to the home of the village doctor. Though he had no formal medical training other than familiarity with standard household cures, the practitioner remained her only hope of aid for her infant or herself. Additionally, she felt required to make a formal report of the death of her husband.

Brusque as usual in his manner, and ignoring the signs of distress apparent in Katrin's appearance, the doctor demanded to know the cause of her husband's death. Afraid to reveal the true circumstances of Kaspar's demise, however, she remained evasive, relating only that her husband had been ill with a fever. Her primary concern at this point was for little Marta. The doctor indicated that he would stop by the next morning.

Meanwhile, at their ostentatious home in another part of town, the Grossveldt household was undergoing its own tribulations. Heinrich had been the first to feel the dire effects, due to his close proximity to Kaspar Schisler. At first the family wasn't sure whether Heinrich's complaints were symptoms of his usual fits of petulance or genuine illness. As the hours passed, however, it became apparent that something very serious was amiss. Spells of coughing, vomiting, and confusion were intermixed with a high fever that stubbornly resisted conventional treatment. Mystified and alarmed, the Grossveldts summoned the town doctor.

Upon examining the boy, the doctor proclaimed that young Heinrich was only suffering from the ague, that there was nothing to be alarmed about. Bed rest and a purgative would soon have him good as new. As he left, the doctor told them, "I'll be back to check on the boy tomorrow morning, after I've seen to the Schisler family. Frau Schisler has informed me that Kaspar passed away, so I will need to fill out the necessary papers before he can be properly buried."

"Kaspar Schisler?" the senior Grossveldt queried in surprise. "I thought he was away from Oberammergau, working in some other village."

"I hadn't heard about that. I only know that his wife came to my place and told me Schisler was dead." With that, he was gone.

Had the doctor observed young Heinrich's response to his announcement of Schisler's death, he might have revised his earlier optimistic diagnosis. No sooner had the boy heard the words than convulsions shook his fevered body and he began to scream uncontrollably, "No, no, I don't want to die like Kaspar Schisler, just for breaking the rules. He made me tell. It's all his fault!"

Mrs. Grossveldt rushed to Heinrich's side, trying to calm the boy. "What is it, my darling? What's wrong? Who made you tell? What do you mean, it's his fault?"

But Heinrich, though bordering on delirium, was still aware enough not to give away the secret of the tunnel. Instead, he continued to scream "No! No! No!" over and over until, exhausted, he drifted into semi-consciousness.

In yet another part of town, Inga Scheerer was feeling uncharacteristically out of sorts. Normally the epitome of exuberant health and good spirits, she found herself sinking into a listless, depressed state totally alien to her usual sunny nature. Her energy level was depleted, and she felt irritable, even toward her good-natured mother.

Her mood brightened a bit when their teacher, Fraulein Waldung, entered the Bake Shop with a cheery greeting for both mother and daughter.

"Good morning, Mrs. Scheerer. Good morning, Inga. My, but you look nice today. Isn't it pleasant to have our village almost back to normal again?"

"Good morning to you, Fraulein Waldung," responded Mrs. Scheerer. "Yes, the mood in town has certainly improved. But it's what we might expect from people of good sense."

"Is there something special we can help you with?" Inga inquired.

"As a matter of fact, I do need a special cake for dessert tonight. Can you help me find something?"

Together, they reviewed the assortment of pastries, selecting one that Fraulein Waldung declared to be just right. Having paid Mrs. Scheerer for her purchase, she gave Inga a warm-hearted embrace, adding,

"Thank you for your assistance, Inga. You're a good girl. I'll be seeing you at school next week."

"You're most welcome, Fraulein Waldung," Inga replied, "and thank *you*. I'm really looking forward to school starting again." She tried to smile with her habitual enthusiasm, but instead lapsed into an abrupt fit of coughing. To make matters worse, the suddenness of the onset left her unable to cover her mouth in time, as both her mother and Fraulein Waldung had always taught her to do. Embarrassment added to the turmoil she was already feeling within.

As soon as her teacher left the shop, Inga gave way to the rush of her emotions. Tears coursed down her velvety cheeks, and she stamped her foot in frustration at the unaccustomed misery she was enduring.

"Why Inga, sweetheart, what's wrong?" her mother asked, surprised by the outburst of temper. "Are you sure you're alright?" She gathered her beautiful daughter into her arms with heartfelt affection.

Sensing something peculiar, Mrs. Scheerer placed her hand on Inga's forehead. Immediately, she stepped back. "My goodness, Inga, you're burning up! No wonder you're not acting like yourself. We need to get you to bed, right now."

At that moment, Rolf entered the shop, in quest of his daily delicacy. Mrs. Scheerer turned to him gratefully. "Oh Rolf, I'm so glad you're here. Would you mind looking after the shop for a few minutes? Inga isn't feeling well, and I need to get her upstairs and put her to bed."

That Inga could ever be ill seemed to astonish Rolf, who was accustomed to seeing her only in perpetual good health. He looked at the exquisite young woman with anxious unease, dismayed to know that she was experiencing discomfort of any kind. Then, responding belatedly to her mother's request, he replied. "Why, of course, Mrs. Scheerer, I'll be happy to watch the shop for you. You just take good care of Inga." Moving closer to Inga, he added in gentle tones, "I'm so very sorry you're not feeling well. I really am." The look in his eyes attested to the sincerity of his concern.

Recompense

Inga again did her best to respond with a sparkling smile, trying to reassure him. "Don't worry about me, Rolf, I'll be fine by tomorrow." But her distress remained obvious as she followed her mother up the stairs.

After a short time, Mrs. Scheerer reappeared. "Thank you so much for staying, Rolf," she told him. "Now, before you go, Inga would like to see you for a bit." She saw the young man's look of surprise. "It's all right," she assured him. "Inga just said there was something she needed to tell you."

Unsure and apprehensive, the youth made his way up the stairs. "In here, Rolf," he heard Inga call from her bedroom, and he made his hesitant way toward the sound of her voice.

Propped up on daintily embroidered pillows in her stately brass bed, a floral comforter drawn up to her shoulders, Inga looked more like an angelic vision to Rolf than an invalid. She motioned to the reticent young man to come closer. "Here, sit on my bed."

Tentatively, Rolf took a seat, though he still appeared uncomfortable. "What is it, Inga? Your mother said you wanted to tell me something."

"I do, Rolf, but I'm not sure I can say it right." She glanced away, uncertain how to proceed.

Then she looked up, directly into Rolf's eyes, with an expression more intense than he had ever seen before. "Please don't stop me until I've finished, Rolf, because what I have to say is very important. You see, even though this all happened so fast, I know that I'm really sick. I didn't want to worry Mother, but I know I've never felt anything like this before. And with all of the bad things going around, like the plague and everything, I'm afraid that what I've caught could be something very serious."

She saw the instant alarm on Rolf's face, and cut off his protest by placing her fingers over his lips. "No, please let me finish," she urged. "I hope you can believe that I'm not trying to be dramatic or anything. It's just that, if something bad should happen to me, I want you to know that I've always had very special feelings for you, Rolf." A tinge of color crept into her cheeks, but she went on. "In fact, in my dreams I always hoped that someday, when we grew up, we'd be married and live happily ever after, just like in the fairytales." She laughed lightly to hide her embarrassment, but her eyes told him she meant every word.

Again she cut him off with her light touch. "I'm telling you all of this, Rolf, because now I'm afraid it can never be. But no matter what happens, I want you always to remember what I just said."

Tears welled in the young man's eyes, both at Inga's tender revelation and at the finality with which she viewed the outcome of her illness. He had never before demonstrated his affection for her, but now he clutched her close to himself, stroking her golden tresses, telling her insistently, "No, Inga, no, nothing bad can happen to you. You're going to be all right again. You just *have* to be." He drew back, looking intently into her eyes. "I don't know what I'd do if you weren't here, Inga. What you said about us makes me feel so happy! But I can't stay happy if I think you aren't well. So please, please don't say any more about not getting better again."

The look of profound young love reflected in the deep azure of Inga's eyes penetrated to Rolf's innermost being. Again he drew the stunning girl to him. When he finally released her, she dropped back on her pillows, a soft smile of serene contentment on her beautiful face.

A sudden fit of coughing racked Inga's delicate frame, breaking the tender mood. She held a lacy handkerchief to her mouth and tried to signal Rolf not to worry, but the cough persisted. Thoroughly frightened, the youth squeezed her free hand and told her, "I'll go get your mother, Inga. She'll know what to do to help."

Despite their best efforts, however, they found that there was actually very little they could do. As Inga's temperature continued to rise, the rasping cough worsened, accompanied by convulsive shudders. Although the young woman maintained an uncomplaining outward stoicism, the gravity of her unrelenting affliction persisted.

Recompense

At Mrs. Scheerer's behest, Rolf hurried to the doctor's house to see if the practitioner could come and provide some assistance. The doctor was not at home, however, evidently engaged with one of the other emergencies that had so unexpectedly struck their village.

Leaving a note requesting the doctor to come as quickly as possible, Rolf returned to the Bake Shop to see if there was some way, *any* way, that he could help to alleviate Inga's discomfort. He felt relief for the moment when Mrs. Scheerer said that Inga had finally drifted off into a restless sleep.

"There doesn't seem to be much more we can do right now," Mrs. Scheerer informed him, but he could detect the depth of her concern. "We'll just hope that she can get some rest before the doctor comes." Embracing the youth with a warmth normally reserved only for her daughter, she continued, "You're truly a fine boy, Rolf, and very dear to my Inga, as you must know. Thank you very much for being here today. But now you'd better be on your way home before your mother starts to worry. And get some rest yourself. We certainly don't want *you* getting sick too, do we?"

Chapter XVI

Now the magnitude of the threat facing Oberammergau became apparent, step by fateful step.

It began when the doctor appeared at the Schisler home the next morning and asked to examine the body of the unfortunate Kaspar. The young widow, barely able to function and helpless to stem the disorder ravaging her baby, led the doctor to the bedroom where her husband's body still lay on the bed. The discolored nodes were clearly visible, but the doctor insisted that Katrin completely strip the corpse to allow a more thorough inspection.

The instant the underclothes were removed, the doctor stepped back, aghast. What he saw was a mass of dark, ulcerated swellings in the groin area, abscessed and festering to the point of turning portions of Kaspar's body into a bloody, misshapen mass.

"This man was carrying...the...the *plague!*" the doctor sputtered in disbelief. "He has brought the dreaded plague into our village!"

Katrin gasped, fully recognizing the significance of the doctor's diagnosis~for her children, for herself, for all of the townspeople of Oberammergau. No news could have been more terrible or more terrifying. Already stricken in body, her spirit now surrendered all hope as well, and she slumped numbly to the floor.

Little Johann, the only member of the family who appeared so far to have escaped the insidious infection, ran to his fallen mother. Putting

Recompense

his arms about her as best he could, he cried, "Mama! Mama! Get up! Please get up, Mama! Marta needs you!"

Ignoring the inert form of the widow at his feet, as well as the anguished cries of the children, the doctor screamed over and over, "What has he done? What has he done?" Then he fled from the house, shrieking, "All who hear my voice, beware. You are in grave danger! Come, we must tell the Burgermeister. He must hear of this at once!"

In the throes of his melancholy fright, the doctor had forgotten his promise to revisit the Grossveldt home that morning to see how young Heinrich was doing. So it was that the slaughterhouse owner and his family were undergoing their difficulties with no outside assistance, no one to help ease their concerns. The Grossveldts had always remained socially aloof, and now there were neither friends nor neighbors to call upon.

Heinrich's condition had steadily worsened during the night, and by morning dark fearsome nodules had appeared on his body. The boy was reduced to moaning wildly in pain, as his horrified parents did everything they knew to try to alleviate his suffering.

Their concern was doubled when Ursula, too, began to complain, first of a blinding headache, then of dizziness and disorientation, and finally of agony coursing unabated throughout her system. When a burning fever materialized as well, her parents could only look at each other in silent, knowing commiseration. Though they did not openly acknowledge it, both recognized that Ursula was now also undergoing the initial phases of the malady their town had tried so desperately to avoid. The situation seemed to have become one completely without hope.

The elder Grossveldt, after trying unsuccessfully to comfort his wife, at last set forth to locate the missing physician and insist that he appear. Approaching the Town Square, he was astonished by the unexpected commotion he encountered. It was not unlike what had occurred following the appearance of the itinerant peddler. Townspeople were once again in wild disorder, some rushing about, some shouting, some engaged in heated debate, while others merely stood by, weeping silently.

Grossveldt grabbed the arm of a passing man. "What's going on here?" he demanded. "What's happening? Has our town gone mad again?"

The accosted citizen, eager to share his dramatic information, turned to Grossveldt. "You mean you don't know? You haven't heard? It's the plague, man, the ghastly plague! It's been brought to our village. Now *all* of us are doomed!" With that, he pulled from Grossveldt's grasp and hastened on to spread his macabre news to any who may not yet have heard.

It was too much for Grossveldt. Not only were his deepest fears confirmed, but now all would demand to know who was responsible for this momentous disaster. Would they try to blame his Heinrich? Did they already know what was afflicting him? Who could have told them? Surely it could not be Heinrich's fault! Someone else must have brought in the plague~perhaps some Jew, who had passed it on to Heinrich. And now his own dear boy was in deathly peril. He must locate the Burgermeister at once and find out what he intended to do about all this.

As he entered the Town Square, the businessman noted a small circle of men, detached from the milling throng, absorbed in animated conversation. At its center was the Burgermeister, who appeared to be addressing most of his remarks to the village doctor. Grossveldt pushed his way toward the group, pleased to have located the two individuals from whom he would demand answers, immediately.

"I've been looking for you, Herr Docktor," he broke in, "and what do I find? A town that has once again lost its senses. May I ask what is going on here?" He glanced around at the group, trying to dramatize the significance of his presence.

The Burgermeister turned and addressed him politely, despite the rudeness of the interruption. "It seems we have an emergency on our hands, Herr Grossveldt. Since you've been looking for our esteemed doctor, perhaps he should explain it for you."

Recompense

∞

The doctor cleared his throat. "I'm afraid it's not good news, Herr Grossveldt. The illness that your Heinrich complained of, well, it seems it may not have been as simple as we thought. In fact…." He paused, unable to meet the businessman's penetrating gaze. Again he cleared his throat, then continued, "In fact, Herr Grossveldt, I fear that your boy may well have come down with…uh…the plague."

Grossveldt stood frozen, his face drained of color, his body sagging. So everybody did know! And they were going to blame Heinrich. The shame would be too great! Surely his precious son could not be held responsible.

Taken aback, Grossveldt's recourse was a resort to bluster. "No, no, Herr Docktor, that cannot be. My boy has a fever, that's all, but it will soon pass. You'll see. Please, don't even speak of anything so terrible as the plague. Don't try to lay blame for such a disaster at *my* door." The sinking sensation he felt inside, however, would not go away.

The Burgermeister intervened. "We're not blaming you or your Heinrich for anything, Herr Grossveldt, but what the doctor says is unfortunately true. The plague *is* in our village. Kaspar Schisler has gone on to his reward, and his body has been examined by our doctor. There can be no doubt that Schisler died of the plague. How he infected your son, we'll probably never know. And how he was able to enter our village we may never know either. What we do know is that he brought the plague in with him. That is the sad truth."

"But what about the guards? And the fires? Weren't they supposed to protect us?" Grossveldt protested. "How could Schisler possibly have got past them? "

The town officials merely shook their heads, no one having the answer. Then Grossveldt remembered: What was it that Heinrich had been crying out in his delirium? He said that something had been "Kaspar Schisler's fault." What had he meant? Had there been some secret connection between the two? Afraid to voice his suspicions, the elder Grossveldt nevertheless recognized their dire implications.

Abruptly leaving the group, he hurried toward his home, wondering how he could possibly relay the dreadful confirmation to his anxious wife. Not only Heinrich, but Ursula, too, had likely been infected, and that did not bode well for his wife or for himself. Obviously, the doctor had no cure, so they could do nothing now but await their fate. Though Kaspar Schisler was dead, Grossveldt knew that the disease was not always fatal to all. "Please God," he prayed as he rushed along, "let my beloved boy and my dear Ursula be spared. Oh God, you *must!*"

Meanwhile, when Rolf awoke that morning, his first thought was that he needed to find out if Inga was feeling better. He dressed as hurriedly as he could, a variety of scenarios, both good and bad, running alternately through his mind. When he came out into their tidy kitchen his mother was not at her usual early morning task, busily preparing breakfast. Instead, he found a note on the table: "Rolf, my customer needed the dress I've been working on right away. I'll be back as soon as I can. Be sure to eat something. I love you, Mother."

After a hasty breakfast of bread and jam and a glass of milk, Rolf wrote his own note: "Mother, I'm going to see how Inga is today, Love, Rolf." Then he rushed off to the Bake Shop.

The first indication that all was not well was the sign in the shop window: "Closed today due to illness." It was a most unusual occurrence for a business that could be depended upon always to serve its customers reliably.

Perplexed, Rolf went around to the back door. Through the window he could see Mrs. Scheerer working in her kitchen, but he could also detect at a glance the deep anxiety on her face. He knocked lightly so as not to disturb Inga. When Mrs. Scheerer appeared, her demeanor made it obvious that his worst fears were about to be confirmed.

"Good morning, Mrs. Scheerer. I'm sorry to bother you so early, but I really need to know how Inga is this morning?"

Recompense

Mrs. Scheerer gave a heavy sigh, managing a wan smile. "You're no bother at all, Rolf, I'm very glad you came by." Then all semblance of a smile faded. "But I'm afraid the news is not good today. Inga seems to be much worse. She has a very high fever, and now when she coughs it makes her throw up. I'm boiling water for some tea, hoping maybe she'll be able to keep that down." The distraught mother was close to tears. "I do wish that doctor would hurry. He still hasn't come by to check on her."

"I'm so sorry, Mrs. Scheerer. I'll go back to the doctor's house right away and see if I can get him to come with me." Rolf paused, looking pleadingly at her, then asked quietly, "But could I please see Inga for just a minute before I go? I won't wake her up or anything, but I'd just like to see her." The look in his eyes spoke more eloquently than any further words he might have uttered.

Mrs. Scheerer hugged the young man and gave his cheek an affectionate pat. "Of course, Rolf, go right on up, but only for a little while. She's a very sick girl, but I'm sure she's awake and would like very much to see you, too." Once more she attempted a brave smile.

Quietly ascending the stairs, Rolf tip-toed to Inga's bedroom. The door was ajar, and he saw the young woman slumped back on her pillows. She was, however, only a specter of the vivacious, vibrant Inga he had always known. Her eyes were closed and her distinctive blonde hair clung damply to her flushed, perspiring face. An involuntary gasp escaped Rolf as he noted the enormity of the change.

Alerted by the sound, Inga opened her eyes. For a moment they reflected disbelief. Then, from some reservoir of inner strength came a smile of such genuine tenderness that Rolf forgot all self-restraint. He dropped to his knees beside her bed and gathered the fragile young woman into his arms, tears coursing down his cheeks. "Inga, Inga," he whispered, "I'm so very sorry you're so sick. We *have* to find a way to help you get better. I promised your mother I'd try again to find the doctor, but I just had to see you first. I'll go now. But I'll never, never forget what you told me. Never!"

He kissed her tenderly on the forehead, his alarm heightened anew by the intensity of the fever radiating from her. With a last look of fathomless devotion, he moved softly from her room.

Returning to the kitchen, he said gently, "Thank you for letting me see her, Mrs. Scheerer. She's really sick, like you said. But I'll run and get the doctor now. He'll know what to do, won't he?" All of his hopes and fears echoed in the anxious question.

"Yes, I'm sure he will. Thank you for being so helpful, Rolf." She tried again to smile, but with little success.

The village doctor was just returning from his conference with the Burgermeister when Rolf reached his house. A look of deep annoyance crossed his face at the realization that yet another individual was in need of his services.

"What is it you want, young man?" he asked sharply. "Don't tell me someone else has caught it!"

"Mrs. Scheerer needs you to come to her place right away, Herr Docktor. Inga is very sick, and we don't know what to do." In spite of the doctor's intimidating manner, Rolf was desperate. "What is it you think she might have caught?"

"Why, the plague, of course! Don't you know the plague has come to our town, in spite of all our efforts to keep it out? Haven't you heard."

No words could have been more devastating. The plague! The "Black Death!" Mustering what little courage he had remaining, Rolf challenged the doctor: "But you can't know what's wrong until you see Inga, Herr Docktor. Maybe it isn't the plague. Maybe she just has a bad fever. Please, please come see her, won't you? Please!"

Struck by the seriousness of the young man's plea, the doctor relented. "All right, I'll see her, but it will take me a while. You wait here until I get ready." As he stepped to his front door, he added as an afterthought, "We can only pray that she hasn't had any contact with that young Schisler family lately. If she has, I'm afraid there can be little hope."

The physician's parting words rang in Rolf's ears. The Schisler family? He knew that Inga went there often to help Mrs. Schisler with the children. But what did that have to do with her illness? How could that have any connection with the plague? He didn't understand.

When the doctor reemerged from his house, he was almost unrecognizable. He was wearing a long, loose robe that covered him from head to toe. Additionally, he wore large protective gloves and a hat. Around his face he had wrapped several layers of cloth, as though to serve as a filter against "miasmas" in the air. In his hand he carried a wooden wand, much like one a magician might use to cast a healing spell.

Noting the quizzical look on Rolf's face, the doctor appeared to feel the need to explain. "I told you that the plague has come to Oberammergau. This is the only means I have to protect myself from its evil force. Even this may be too late, after what I encountered at the Schisler house." He turned and strode swiftly down the street, calling back to Rolf, "Come, come, let's get on with it if we must."

At the Bake Shop, Mrs. Scheerer welcomed the doctor solemnly and led him to her daughter's room. It was then Rolf saw the purpose of the wand. The physician refused to touch the patient, choosing instead to remove the covers and do his probing only with the stick. But even such a cursory examination led to the inevitable conclusion.

"I'm afraid the news is not good, Frau Scheerer," he informed the anxious mother. "Your daughter has definitely contracted the plague, from what source I do not know. But she is not the first in our town to be stricken."

"Oh no, no, she can't have the plague! Please don't say that, Herr Docktor," Mrs. Scheerer protested. "My Inga is all I have. She has a fever, but nothing like the plague. You know our town has been protected from that. It *can't* be here in Oberammergau."

The practitioner shook his head. "I'm very sorry, Frau Scheerer, but your daughter does have the disease, of that I am certain. Our efforts have not been successful. The plague has reached us in spite of all we have done to keep it away."

Mrs. Scheerer covered her face with her hands, her entire being shuddering with uncontrollable sobs.

"As to your daughter," the doctor continued, "you can either stay here with her and try to make her more comfortable, or you can leave her and try to save yourself. Either way, your Inga is going to die. The plague shows very little mercy, Frau Scheerer. Your daughter is gravely ill. She will die!"

With that, he turned and left the shop.

Chapter XVII

Inexorably, the death toll began to mount in Oberammergau. The Schisler family had been only the earliest victims~husband, wife, and baby Marta. Miraculously, little Johann had somehow avoided infection and was now being cared for in the home of his uncle.

In the days following, it became apparent that few would escape the insidious disease. The entire Grossveldt family perished. The senior Grossveldt managed to survive almost a week longer than the others, but finally he too expired, isolated and alone.

Mrs. Scheerer's Bake Shop remained closed, the sign in the window bearing mute testimony to the torment of both body and spirit going on within. The mother continued to watch helplessly as her cherished daughter faded under the plague's vicious onslaught. Though her ministrations brought brief moments of temporary relief to Inga, they also led to extended exposure for Mrs. Scheerer, and ultimately she succumbed as well.

Fraulein Waldung, busy with her preparations for the new school term, found her strength and energy gradually ebbing. Before she could determine the cause, the plague had fixed its deathly grip on her, and she joined the list of unfortunate casualties.

The village priest, maintaining faith with his trusting flock, insisted upon administering last rites to any townspeople who requested his services. The modicum of comfort he was able to provide in this way seemed to him ample reward for the dangers that such close association presented. In the end, his faithfulness brought about his demise.

An unprecedented dilemma arose as these and other citizens of Oberammergau fell prey to the rampaging epidemic during the ensuing days. Fear of contamination led to refusal by those who customarily provided burial services at the local cemetery to continue to provide assistance. As a result, unburied bodies became a major potential calamity for the beleaguered village.

It was Herman the blacksmith who came forward in this crisis, despite the obvious dangers to himself. "These good people~our friends, our neighbors~deserve a decent Christian burial," he insisted stubbornly. With no one else willing to help, Herman took upon himself the solitary, arduous task of gathering up the bodies of any new victims, transporting them to the cemetery, reciting a brief scripture over them, and commending them to their final earthly resting place.

It was inevitable, in the process of this humanitarian undertaking, that the blacksmith should end up being stricken himself. In spite of the debilitating effects of the pestilence, ignoring the personal pain, Herman continued at his task until finally he too collapsed, ready to join the procession of death. Now it was up to the town fathers to find some means to fill the void.

On the day Rolf returned to his home following his final visit with Inga, he had found that his mother was still away, busy with her dressmaking duties. As he waited, the young man became increasingly conscious that something was wrong, that something sinister was affecting his own sense of well-being. Ever since he had awakened, his eyes had been burning, his head throbbing in a manner totally contrary to his customary feelings of general good health. He had attributed the malaise to his deep concern about Inga's illness, but now the pain began to intensify beyond belief. His face felt hot and sweaty, and the turbulent restiveness in his stomach added to his unease.

Recompense

Rolf knew instinctively the fatal course upon which he was embarked. Having seen Inga's symptoms and suffering left him without a shred of doubt that he, too, had become infected. Now it was only a matter of waiting for the end.

As the finality of his fate settled into inescapable reality, Rolf began to formulate one fixed, unalterable determination: somehow, by some means, he must keep the deadly contagion from spreading to his mother. How he would manage this feat in his own weakened state he wasn't sure. But one thing he did resolve~that he personally would not become the instrument of her death.

For a few minutes he remained listless, incapable of rational thought, as he attempted to escape the heightening torment by retreating inwardly, through transcendental transference, to a locale where pain was unreal and unknown. Briefly, he was successful and felt a relaxing nothingness overtake him. But then, by sheer power of will, he forced himself back to total consciousness. He would never be able to devise his plan of protection if he were adrift in some ethereal sphere.

Slowly, with absolute certainty, Rolf concluded what he must do. Without further hesitation, he compelled his tortured body to proceed with the necessary preparations.

First, he gathered such food and drink as would be essential for his solitary confinement~some bread, cheese, fruit, a bit of sausage, as well as a container of water and a large glass of milk. These he carried to his small bedroom, arranging them carefully on a shelf usually reserved for his few books and knick-knacks. Candles and a chamber-pot were already in place, and a spare blanket lay folded across the foot of his wooden bed.

Next, he crumpled up the earlier note he had left on the table for his mother, replacing it with a new one: "Dearest Mother, I've just come from Inga's house. The doctor said she has the plague. I'm certain I'm getting it too, so I want to make really sure I don't give it to you. That's why I'm staying in my room from now on. I have food and drinks, so try not to worry. I love you very, very much! Your son, Rolf."

Looking around to make sure he had covered all contingencies, he next securely locked his door and lowered into place a sturdy bar he had once fashioned while playing "make-believe castle" in his room. Finally, he closed and locked the shutters covering his only window, cutting off all access from outside. He had effectively turned his bedroom into a reclusive, sequestered stronghold.

It wasn't long before he heard his mother return home, humming as she bustled about the kitchen. Then came a long, silent pause when Rolf assumed she must be reading his note. He heard a sharp cry, followed by the sound of his mother's hurried footsteps approaching his bedroom door. She tried the latch, then pushed on the door, but quickly appeared to realize that his room was thoroughly secured.

A growing comprehension of what Rolf intended to do seemed to parallel his mother's recognition of her own helplessness. Her distressed cry gave voice to the depth of the dilemma. "Rolf, Rolf, my darling boy, please open the door! Please, Rolf! If you're sick, I want to help you. I'm sure you can't have anything as serious as the plague. I'll get the doctor to come examine you. Please, Rolf, open the door."

The agony in her voice was so intense that Rolf could feel tears begin to spill from his eyes. He hadn't intended to cause such deep hurt to the person he loved above all others. And yet, precisely because she was so dear to him, his determination to save her from the horrible fate to which the plague would condemn her became even more firm.

"Mother, please don't be so sad," he began. "I just *can't* let you in, because if I do, I know you'll get sick, too. I think that's how Inga caught the illness, from taking care of the Schisler children. And the doctor said Kaspar Schisler died of the plague."

Recompense

༜

"But Rolf, that doesn't mean *you* have the plague," his mother interrupted. "You're probably just not feeling well, that's all. Please let me in so that I can take care of you. Please, Rolf!"

Momentarily Rolf hesitated, considering what his mother had just said. Maybe she was right. Maybe this was only a temporary spell of not feeling well, and soon everything bad would go away. Maybe Inga would get better, too, and his life would be back to normal. It was a tempting, alluring notion.

Then Rolf's resolve returned, bolstered by the understanding that he *knew* nothing could ever again be as it had been before. Inga was dying, the doctor had said, and Rolf could feel in his own body the steady incursion of some unusual, terrible sickness. He must keep his mother safe, no matter how desperately she pleaded. He simply could not open that door.

"Mother, I'm terribly sorry," he told her, "but I *can't* let you in, no matter what happens. I love you too much, Mama, I really don't want you to be harmed. I just can't let you catch what I have. Please, please believe that I *have* to do this." His voice trailed off in a stifled sob.

Knowing Rolf as she did, his mother could sense the absolute determination, bordering on obstinacy, of her son when he set on a course of action. She decided not to press her wishes at this point, but resolved also not to abandon him without exerting every unrelenting effort possible on his behalf.

"All right, Rolf," she concurred, "I won't ask you to open your door now. Promise me that you'll eat something, and try to sleep. I have to go out again, but I'll talk to you when I get back. I love you, son, I love you so much!"

Once more, Rolf felt tears welling in his eyes. "Thank you, Mother. I love you too! Go ahead now and take care of your business. But please try to be careful and not get close to anyone who's sick. I'll be just fine here. I have everything I need."

Though apprehensive and torn, the worried mother was equally firm in her resolution to save her son, no matter what. She left the house and headed directly for the Town Square, watching closely for the one person she felt she could count on in this emergency. Sure enough, as she entered the Square she saw him~engaged in earnest conversation with a fellow townsman as he descended the steps of the Town Hall.

She waited quietly for the two men to complete their discussion, and then approached the Burgermeister. With a polite curtsy she said, "Herr Burgermeister, if you please, may I have a moment of your time? I realize that you have many, many serious concerns facing you right now, but I need your opinion on a critical concern of my own."

The gravity of her demeanor, as well as the anxiety emanating from her expressive eyes, led the official to immediate agreement.

"Of course, of course," he assured her pleasantly, his own host of problems momentarily set aside to deal with the human needs of the woman before him. "Please, come to my office where we can talk without interruption."

Rolf's mother could not recall ever having been in the dignified environs of administrative power represented by the Burgermeister's office. Still, she refused to allow the magisterial surroundings to intimidate her. Instead, she proceeded to explain as clearly as she was able what her son had decided to do, and together Burgermeister and mother reviewed their possible options.

When it became apparent that there was no simple satisfactory solution to the problem, Rolf's mother found courage for one further proposal. Sincerely, whole-heartedly she poured forth the outline of a possible plan, her wide, intense eyes lending credence to its plausibility.

When she had finished, the Burgermeister was silent for a moment, thoughtfully contemplating what had been suggested. Then a slight smile began playing at the corners of his mouth, a glint of hope reflected in his eyes. "Yes, yes, it could be," he said softly. He slapped his hand on his desk, and repeated with genuine excitement, "Yes, it could be!" He rose from behind the desk and began pacing the room animatedly. "I will call a town meeting for tomorrow night, even though people are fearful of congregating in this crisis, and you can place your proposal before the good citizens of Oberammergau." Now he was smiling broadly. "Yes, yes, I think they will accept."

Although deeply pleased with the positive response, Rolf's mother raised her hand to protest. "Excuse me, Herr Burgermeister, thank you for your confidence, but if you please, I think it would be better if *you* make the proposal as your own." She lowered her dark eyes briefly, then continued, "As you know, there are those who resent having a woman meddle in affairs of government. So perhaps you should just explain the plan and then let the people decide." She rose to leave. "Thank you most kindly. And now I must hurry home to my son."

The succeeding hours crept by, with Rolf resolutely maintaining his isolation throughout the night and into the following day. Communication between mother and son consisted solely of hopeful words of encouragement and tender exchanges passed through the barrier of the barred door.

As evening approached, heralding time for the town meeting, only peaceful silence came from Rolf's room. His mother breathed a sigh of relief, thankful that her boy seemed to be experiencing at least temporary escape from his pain through the serenity of sleep. Fearful that she might awaken him, she quietly slipped a note under his door: "My Dear Rolf, I've gone to the town meeting, where the Burgermeister will propose a plan which we hope will halt the plague. Soon you'll be well again, and we can enjoy our lives together as we did before. I love you, my son, Mother."

The meeting opened in an atmosphere of both fear and expectancy. The wide-spread inroads of the deadly pestilence had been felt by almost every family by now, and yet for this one evening panic was being held in abeyance. A rumor had gradually circulated that the Burgermeister had come up with a proposal which offered real hope. Villagers had faith in their leader, and now crowded into the chambers of the Town Hall eager to hear any words that might promise a means of escape from what they had come to believe was their inevitable fate.

Having called the meeting to order, the Burgermeister began with a few opening remarks: "Friends and neighbors, thank you for coming here tonight in spite of the dangers we all know may be inherent in such a gathering. But perilous times call for courageous action. As you know, our village stands in mortal danger. Within the past days, we have lost one of our most successful businessmen and his entire family. We have lost our esteemed bakery proprietor and her daughter. We have lost our blacksmith, our teacher, our revered parish priest, people well-known and loved by all of us. Altogether, we have lost eighty-three of our respected citizens~eighty-three human beings who walked among us and worked among us, and now are no more."

He paused, wiping at his eyes, trying hard to keep control. Then he continued in somber, measured tones, "That is why I have asked you to gather tonight to hear a proposal which may or may not be feasible, but which may well be our last hope for an end to this deadly epidemic." Again he paused, looking directly at Rolf's mother. A surge of momentary alarm flooded through her before the Burgermeister, with a faint smile, returned his gaze to the audience.

"What I am proposing tonight can work *only* if it has the support and blessing of each and every one of you. It must be a total community commitment, carried out in heartfelt honesty and humility if it has any hope of succeeding. What I am suggesting, dear friends and neighbors, represents an appeal to a Power far, far greater than ourselves."

Then he laid out the plan. "I am asking that each of us undertake a sacred covenant with our God. In exchange for an end to the contagion that is currently decimating our beloved hamlet, we will all take a solemn vow: in the coming year, we will present for all to see a miracle play, or passion play, depicting the last week of the life of Christ on earth. By demonstrating on a public stage the agony and triumph of our Lord, we will be affirming our eternal gratitude for His love and compassion toward us.

"It will require that you, beloved citizens of Oberammergau, study the Word of God and then yourselves depict the roles of the various Biblical characters involved. Assignments will be made based on who is best able to portray the spirit of their chosen character. Obviously, selection of the person who will play the role of Christ will be most difficult, since that individual will be responsible for exemplifying not only His glorious message of love, but also His suffering and death, and finally His resurrection and ascension. All this we will pledge to do as an offering of thanks for God's mercy in sparing our village from further devastation."

A long moment of silence greeted the Burgermeister's proposal, as each villager carefully considered what had just been suggested. Would the plan work? No one knew. They were, after all, making a covenant with God. Could they do what had been proposed? Again they weren't sure. But one thing did appear certain: it would be far better than having no plan at all. Directed, positive action must surely be superior to resignation into hopeless despair.

A scattering of applause broke the silence, at first tentative and hesitant, then rising into a sustained crescendo of approval. The Burgermeister looked around at his townspeople, a happy smile of gratification playing across his face, his head nodding in satisfaction. Finally he raised his hand for quiet.

"Thank you, my people, thank you," he said, tears glistening in his eyes. "Now, do you have any questions, or comments? Remember, this is a most sacred undertaking, not to be entered into lightly. If there are reservations, please express them before you make such a serious commitment."

A hand was raised, and one of the villagers asked, "Are we sure that we would be doing enough? After all, we are asking a great deal from our Heavenly Father, and perhaps He will require more of us than just one presentation of our Lord's death and resurrection."

Nods of assent greeted this comment, and for a time various additional commitments or possibilities were weighed, with no unanimity of opinion emerging.

Then Rolf's mother rose from her seat, looking around almost apologetically before making her suggestion: "If you please, shouldn't we make sure that our thanks to our God is ongoing, something that our children and our children's children will remember? If the plague does end and our village is spared, could we commit ourselves to presenting this portrayal of the passion of Christ not just once, but on a *regular* basis? Could we repeat it, perhaps, maybe every ten years? Would that be asking too much?" She lowered her eyes and sat down quickly, her cheeks flushing with color.

Cries of "Yes!" "Yes!" "Good!" came from various parts of the room, and everywhere heads nodded in agreement with this last proposal.

The Burgermeister rapped sharply on the table, his eyes sparkling. "Are we ready to put this to an official vote?" Throughout the audience, heads nodded once again.

But then he hesitated, and for a moment he was silent, deep in thought. At last, in earnest tones, he voiced an additional proposition: "Since we are undertaking a sacred covenant with God Almighty, would it not be more appropriate to make our vow in our parish church, before the High Alter, the Alter of the Cross? Would that not help to demonstrate for all the solemnity with which we undertake this oath?"

Recompense

Once more the townspeople of Oberammergau agreed, and a quiet exodus ensued, with citizens proceeding in a dignified but hopeful march to the village church.

As soon as everyone was inside and the audience had been called to order, the Burgermeister posed the momentous question: "All those who sincerely commit themselves to carry out our solemn oath, both now and for the future, say 'Aye'." The roar was deafening. "Opposed?" Silence.

The official was too moved to speak. Tears welled in his eyes. He surveyed the gathered villagers slowly, deliberately. Then, clearing his throat, he stated in a strong, firm voice, "Citizens, our decision, and our commitment, is unanimous. God willing, Oberammergau will be saved!"

Cheers echoed through the house of worship as the inhabitants milled about, talking excitedly, gesturing, slapping each other on the back. In their minds the town had been brought back from the abyss, and once more they felt they had true reason for hope. They believed deeply in their relation with their God and trusted in His ability to accept their solemn pledge and act on their behalf.

What they did not know, and could not have known~neither Burgermeister, nor citizens, nor loving mother~was that in a locked and barred bedroom on a quiet side street in a modest home in their quaint little village, the relentless plague had already claimed its eighty-fourth victim.

Chapter XVIII

Like a whisper echoing through a long empty tunnel, Brandon St. Clair heard the hushed voice asking softly, "Brandon, are you all right?" Overtones of anxious urgency made the question more compelling, like a summons that could not be ignored.

Slowly opening his eyes, not sure if he was asleep, awake, or in a world somewhere in between, Brandon began to survey his surroundings. On the stage in front of him, the closing scene of the Passion Play was unfolding. Elegantly robed choir members fanned out wide on each side of the stage, while the center was occupied by characters from the drama hailing the risen Christ, triumphant over the cross, holding aloft his banner of victory. Uplifting music enhanced the aura of conquest. It was a glorious, moving scene, a fitting end to an enactment of thanksgiving faithfully reaffirmed throughout the years.

Seated directly in front of him, Brandon noticed Margaret Wilson. She was reaching into the small camera bag beneath her chair for her zoom lens, while at the same time trying to keep her attention focused on the concluding performance. To the left, his glance took in another couple from their tour group, people he recognized but had not got to know very well. The wife was dabbing at her moist eyes with a Kleenex, while the husband had joined a host of others in the audience taking snapshots of the closing scene, everyone having been informed earlier that this was the only portion of the production where photos were allowed.

Recompense

∞

As he turned to his right, Brandon saw Father Hochburg studying him intently, the quizzical expression on his face denoting both curiosity and concern. Once more the priest whispered his question, "Are you all right?" Brandon nodded, trying to smile, but the sense of unreality remained.

A sudden chill penetrated Brandon, bringing on an involuntary shudder, as he recalled the vividness of what he had just experienced. He knew with incontrovertible certainty that in the events he had witnessed in Old Oberammergau, particularly the death of young Rolf, he had been a part of circumstances that were immensely personal, though he knew of no way to account for what had actually happened. He shivered again, as Father Hochburg continued his watchful scrutiny. However, the thoughtful priest did not press for an explanation, though his eyes clearly indicated bewilderment.

With the same intuitive insight that had made him aware of his mystical connection to Rolf, Brandon now sensed a further phenomenon: he *knew*, with incontrovertible certainty, that *somehow* the recurring sequences of headache agony were ended. It was as though an oppressive burden had been lifted~how, he had no idea. All he knew was that a lightness, an overwhelming sense of well-being, had replaced the constant threat of recent weeks, and he drew in a long breath of thankful relief.

The crowd filed from the theater, some happily trading comments about the performance, others going quietly as though pondering its deeper significance. Brandon was among the latter, his thoughts still in turmoil as he tried to sort out what had been happening. When Father Hochburg clapped him on the shoulder in parting, adding a cheery "See you at dinner," he merely nodded and smiled, still locked in his own thoughts.

During dinner at their hotel that evening Brandon remained unusually quiet, though he listened attentively to the give-and-take review occurring between Father Hochburg and Margaret, seated across from him. "It was definitely a worthwhile presentation," Margaret concluded, "but still very traditional and predictable. I didn't detect any new philosophical truths or ideologies."

"That's just the point," the priest responded. "It's supposed to be a drama presented to give *thanks*, not to provide some new theological interpretation. It's the way they've been doing this for centuries. They're sincere about what they do, and I don't think they've forgotten why the whole presentation was initiated."

On this point both agreed, and they continued their exchange of ideas while they dined with obvious pleasure. Brandon, meanwhile, picked at his food and made an early excuse to return to his room. He needed more time for reflection before he was ready to share the unnerving occurrences of the afternoon with anyone.

The next day was a "free day" in Oberammergau for the tourist group, their last before they returned to Munich and prepared for the flight home. For many of the travelers, with their adventure so near an end, the day provided a final opportunity to browse through the enticing wood-carving shops of the village, seeking last minute gifts or mementos of their trip. For others, it meant a day to "experience" their Bavarian environment by strolling the ancient streets, or simply by passing the time sipping coffee at one of the outdoor cafes.

At breakfast, Brandon was joined by Father Hochburg, who was still on an emotional high from finally having observed the famous Passion Play. "Well Brandon," he began as he juggled his amply-filled breakfast plate and a glass of orange juice, "what do you plan to do today for an encore? I can't think of anything that can ward off a giant let-down after yesterday."

Brandon looked up at the genial priest with a smile of genuine welcome. "Won't you join me, Father? I have an idea for at least part of the day, and I really hoped you might go along."

Recompense

Father Hochburg expressed interest. "Great! That's exactly what I wanted to hear. Now, what's on the agenda?"

"Well, this may not sound very up-lifting after yesterday's extravaganza, but what I have in mind is a visit to the local cemetery." The look of surprise on the cleric's face brought a laugh. "Okay, okay, I know we're dealing with a somber subject, but I'm really curious about the people who died from what was called the 'Black Death'. In a way, they gave their lives so that the world could have the gift of this great Passion Play. Maybe we can find some of their gravestones, if they're identified. At least I'd like to give it a try."

For a moment, Father Hochburg considered the prospect. Then he thumped the table in agreement. "You know, that sounds intriguing, Brandon. We might just find some 'deep background' for this whole adventure, if you'll pardon the pun. Besides, it's the best offer I've had. But first, I'd like to make a deal with you."

"Oh? And what might that be?"

"Well, the village cemetery is right at the parish church, as I understand it. So how about this: You attend mass with me first, and then we'll explore the cemetery to our hearts' content."

"You've got a deal! Maybe we'll even have time to see a few of the other sights. I picked up a little map at the hotel, and it shows several things in town that look interesting."

As soon as they had finished breakfast, the two were on their way. "Where to first?" Father Hochburg asked. "We've still got some time before the second mass."

"How about going by 'Pilate's House', or the 'Pilatushaus', as the locals call it? The exterior paintings there are supposed to be outstanding. And it's not much of a detour on our way to church."

Heading down the street from their hotel, they had no problem finding the house with its special decorative paintings. Particularly impressive was the illustration of Christ appearing before Pilate, from which the building had drawn its name.

"Look at that columned balcony and balustrade over the entryway, Brandon," Father Hochburg remarked. "It looks like you could step right out on it, doesn't it?"

"It sure does. According to the notation on the back of my map, all of the art work was done originally by a man named Franz Swinck, back in the 18th Century. The old Bavarian name for this type of painting is 'lòftlmalerei,' whatever that means, and Zwinck was the master. It really is impressive."

"I think it means a kind of 'airy' painting, which would certainly describe what we're looking at. Is the building still used?"

"It's owned by the town now, and used for a variety of things, including a working museum for its handicrafts. But I see it's closed today until later in the afternoon."

Continuing back along the Dorf Strasse, the two men approached the parish church. The steeple bells began to peal, as if in welcome, and they made their way into the sanctuary. Again, as with the Wieskirche they had visited earlier, the modest exterior of the building did not prepare them for what they found inside. While not as large or elaborate as the former, this simple "pfarr kirche", or parish church, nevertheless contained an elegant, ornate marbled high altar, two side altars honoring its namesakes, St. Peter and St. Paul, plus its own stunning ceiling frescoes. Altogether, it created an atmosphere of reverence bordering on awe.

Brandon joined his friend in celebration of the mass, even though he was not familiar with all of the finer points of the ritual. He could readily appreciate the devout sincerity of the participants, and the graceful setting further enhanced the vibrant spirit of worship.

With the service over, Father Hochburg patted Brandon on the shoulder. "Well, that wasn't too bad, was it? Would you mind if I took a few minutes to speak with their priest~that is, if his English is better than my German?"

"Not at all. Go right ahead. I'll look around a bit more. This really is an imposing place."

As he walked slowly toward the rear of the church, Brandon noticed a small ante-room with a religious scene in miniature barely visible through a large glass window. Below it was a metal box with a slot, and a sign requesting a donation of one Deutschmark. Searching through the coins in his pocket, Brandon found the appropriate one and dropped it into the slot. Immediately sections of the scene began to light up, until eventually an entire panorama of intricately carved wooden figurines was revealed, depicting scenes from the life of Christ that coordinated with those of the Passion Play. It was one more example of the skill of the "holzschnitzerei", the woodcarvers' art in Oberammergau, and Brandon made sure that his friend didn't miss it.

Next Brandon and Father Hochburg began their exploration of the cemetery, surrounding three sides of the parish church. Meticulously neat and well-groomed, it contained the widest variety of distinctive grave markers the two had ever seen. Some were wrought iron, ranging from intricate renderings in white and gold to one featuring a large ruby heart. Others were full-sized bronze statues, or traditional granite chronicling some of Oberammergau's most famous citizens. The markers that seemed particularly appropriate to the village and its heritage, however, were the hand-carved wooden ones, frequently featuring the crucified Christ, a constant reminder of the role that religious faith had played in evolvement of the hamlet.

One thing puzzled Brandon as he examined marker after marker: he could find none that went back to the actual time of the plague. The oldest dates appeared to be in the 1700's, a full century later than the onslaught of the "Black Death" which had led the town to make its historic vow.

"Why do you suppose we can't find any graves from the plague era?" he asked the cleric as they continued their inspection.

"It's hard to tell. I suppose they could have been obliterated when the new parish church was built during the 1730's and '40's, although that seems unlikely considering the attentive care they lavish on the current gravesites. I'm as much in the dark as you are, Brandon."

"Let's hope it doesn't indicate a forgetting of the past, or a substituting of current pageantry for the suffering that brought the town its present fame. I'd be disappointed if I thought that was the case."

"I couldn't agree more. But I'm sure that a village like this, which really owes its entire *raison d'etre* to the events of its past, would find it hard to neglect the significance of its heritage. I wish I'd thought to ask the parish priest about it."

"Anyway, I guess we shouldn't let our concerns detract from the honor and esteem for the dead this cemetery reflects in general. Maybe we'll find our answer somewhere else."

"That reminds me," Father Hochburg broke in, "the priest did mention that there's another newer cemetery not far from here. He also said we should be sure to go by 'The Crucifixion Group' on our way, if we decide to go there."

"Sounds great. Did he explain what 'The Crucifixion Group' was?"

"No, he said we could read all about it on the marker attached to the fence. He seemed to think we'd be impressed."

Checking his village map, Brandon quickly located the two sites and the men set out. After a short stroll down Ettaler Strasse, they turned at Konig Ludwig Strasse and headed toward the river. At the corner, just before they reached the bridge, Brandon halted and pointed to his right.

"Look, there's the Hotel BØld that Herta mentioned, where we might have stayed. It looks like a very nice place, too."

Recompense

"Yes, not quite as centrally located as the Alte Post, but obviously very popular. Maybe we can stay there when we come back, about ten years from now," the priest concluded with a chuckle.

On the bridge they stopped again to admire the clear, sparkling Ammer River flowing through the town. "Its banks are so precise it looks like some efficient German engineers *built* that river, doesn't it?" Brandon observed, eliciting another chuckle from Father Hochburg.

They continued their pleasant stroll for some distance, until the road ended in a turn-around. From there a rather steep path took them back and forth, leading upward. Reaching the crest of the prominence, both men realized why the parish priest had felt no need to elaborate about "The Crucifixion Group."

Before them stood an immense, magnificent marble monument, comprised of three figures: Christ on the Cross in the center, Mary on the left, and what appeared to be a representative Apostle on the right. The marker on the wrought-iron fence indicated that the monument had been donated to the village by King Ludwig II in 1875, in gratitude for a performance of the Passion Play he had attended some years earlier. At the time, it had been the largest marble memorial in the world.

The site of the "Kreuzigungs-Gruppe" monument provided a further bonus: an exceptional view of Oberammergau, nestled peacefully in its mountain-ringed valley. As they picked out the various landmarks, such as the Passion Play Theater and the Pfarrkirche, Brandon posed an additional question, based on his observations.

"Father, I'm sure you've noticed the big differences in architectural styles between the Catholic and Protestant churches. Just look at that simple, almost stark spire on the little Lutheran church near the Theater, and then at the imposing steeple with its onion-shaped spire on the parish church. From what I've seen, the differences are even more pronounced inside. Why? Does it have anything to do with their rituals, or styles of worship? After all, they both worship the same God."

"You're right, the structural differences are pretty obvious, especially here in Bavaria. But it really goes back a long way, to the time of the Reformation."

"Oh? How's that?"

"Well, at the time of the Reformation, that was one of the very things the Protestants were 'protesting' against. They felt the Church had become too wrapped up in its wealth and ostentation, forgetting the real purpose of worship. And they had a point. So they made their break, determined to worship God in a more direct, personal manner, in the simplest of surroundings."

"How did the Catholic Church respond?"

"You mean other than the Thirty Years War, with all of its devastation? The Catholic Church did gradually make a lot of the reforms that had been demanded. But by then it was too late, and the split had become final. So the Catholics engaged in a 'Counter-Reformation', determined to keep their rituals as well as their ornate houses of worship, almost flaunting their wealth and tradition in opposition to the austerity of the Protestants. Today it sounds kind of petty, but at that time it was taken very seriously."

"Is that when the elaborate Rococo style we saw at the Wieskirche became so popular?"

"Yes, it is. It's pretty hard to get more 'showy' than *that* to make your point, wouldn't you agree?" Father Hochburg finished with a laugh.

By now they had made their leisurely way from the monument park, following a small trail curving back toward town along the wooded base of the Kofelberg. It was a delightful walk, and they stopped frequently to admire the natural beauty of their surroundings.

Eventually the trail dropped down from the woods and they arrived at the New Cemetery, which exhibited the same respectful care and tidiness they had witnessed at the church. After looking around briefly, again finding no memorials to those who had perished in the distant past, they followed a path that took them back close to the Ammer River.

Then Brandon spotted it! He had been looking around, enjoying the ambiance of the area, when he saw a stele-like monument ahead, standing between converging paths.

"That looks interesting, Father. Shall we check it out?"

"Sure! We wouldn't want to miss anything."

As they approached the square concrete pillar with its molded bronze top, the two men realized they had finally found what they had been searching for.

"Look, Brandon," Father Hochburg called out, excitement ringing in his voice. "It's a monument to the victims of the plague!"

Both circled the pillar, appreciatively studying the small bronze figures representing those who had lost their lives back before the vow was taken.

"Wow! They really didn't forget!" Brandon exclaimed. "See this commemorative inscription? And on this side is the date: 1633."

"My faith is restored," Father Hochburg intoned, only half in jest.

It was a fulfilling moment, resulting partly from the thrill of discovery, but mostly from the realization that the residents of the quaint little village had not, after all, forgotten their heritage.

CHAPTER XIX

Both men were profoundly affected by the significance of the memorial monument they had found. They spoke very little as they made their way back toward the Dorf Platz, or Town Square, which Brandon suggested as a site for a late lunch. To him, it seemed an appropriate locale to analyze the day's happenings, since it had served as such a focal point in the historic events surrounding intrusion of the plague epidemic in 1633.

As they waited for their orders to arrive, Father Hochburg broached the subject both had been avoiding. Turning his intent gaze upon Brandon, he asked quietly, "Now, Brandon, are you ready to tell me what was happening to you during the Play yesterday afternoon? Where *were* you? For a while you seemed to be off in a totally different world."

Brandon lowered his eyes, feeling his face begin to flush. He tried to cover his discomfiture with a light laugh. "As I've said before, you certainly are observant, Father. I figured you'd just think I'd gone to sleep." Then he became deeply serious. "But thank you for asking, because it's something I've been wanting to discuss with you, except I wasn't sure just how to approach it."

With that Brandon launched into a full, reflective account of what he had witnessed in Old Oberammergau, stopping briefly only when the waitress arrived to serve their luncheon. As soon as the young woman in her Bavarian costume was gone, he resumed his narration, with the intrigued cleric listening intently, not interrupting despite his many questions.

Recompense

⌘

A long moment of quiet ensued when Brandon completed his story, as both men considered the significance of what had just been recounted. Then Father Hochburg broke the silence. "So, are you saying that Mrs. Scheer, Margaret, Herman, the Grossfeldts, you and I, we *all* lived in another time back in Old Oberammergau? And we all died from the plague? Is that what you're telling me?" His questions were pointed but not hostile, as though he were searching for some logic, some rationale to help him comprehend what he had just heard.

"That's just it," Brandon rejoined. "I'm not really sure *what* was happening. All I know is that you were all there, and I was there, and all of us were exposed to the Black Plague in one way or another, and one by one we died. When young Rolf died, I just *knew* it was me, and that's when my reverie or dream or whatever it was ended. But so far I haven't been able to come up with any kind of explanation that makes sense."

The cleric fidgeted with the cross hanging from his neck, his brow creased deeply as though completely perplexed. "You make it sound almost like some sort of *déjà vu*. Or maybe something more exotic, like time-travel."

"I told you that I can't explain it, Father," Brandon insisted. "I've been racking my brain for an answer. As a lawyer, I've always been taught that there are plausible reasons behind everything that happens"~he stopped, his eyes twinkling briefly, and he added with a laugh, "except maybe behind the decisions of some juries."

But Father Hochburg was not ready to give up the quest. "Are you familiar with the psychological concepts of Carl Jung, Brandon?"

"Only vaguely, from some classes I was required to take in college," Brandon confessed. "Why? Does he have a psychological answer for what happened?"

"No, not exactly. But his ideas of the 'collective unconscious' have always intrigued me and may offer some insights. I'm not sure."

"Fill me in, Father. I'd like to know more."

"Well, according to Jung, our conscious nature is mostly concerned with the *self*, or the *ego*, whereas what he calls the 'collective unconscious' is more reflective of the individual's relationship to *all* of society, or to the whole human community in general. Okay so far?"

"Yes, go on."

"It seems some have interpreted all of this to mean there are 'collective memories' as well, memories of what the human community has experienced in the past. These memories are passed down subconsciously, and are present in the mind of each individual, at least in part. We may not even be aware of them until some event, some occurrence, triggers them. Then we become conscious of them, even if we can't logically determine how or why."

"Hmmm. That is an interesting concept. Would that mean that my *subconscious* made me experience something that happened long ago in all of our lives, even though we're all very much here in the present?"

"I suppose it's possible. Does it sound at all reasonable to you?"

"In a way, I guess. And that could also tie in to a *broader* idea that I've had for a long time. Actually, you could say the idea is my philosophy of religion. Are you ready for this?" Brandon asked with a chuckle.

The affable priest raised his hands in mock surrender. "No, but I'm sure you're going to lay it on me anyway, so go ahead." He smiled broadly. "I told you that you'd make a fine 'member of the cloth', remember?"

"Okay then, here goes. Now, what if Jung's 'collective unconscious' is really *more* than just common memories or experiences? What if it's the very essence of what we call God, or the Divine?"

"How do you mean?"

"Remember the old Transcendentalists, like Emerson and Thoreau? They believed in something they called the 'Over-Soul', which to them represented the Supreme Being. They felt that each of us as individuals had a bit of that Over-Soul in us. It was our duty to bring our *personal* souls back into communion with the Over-Soul, first by perfecting our-selves and then gradually by perfecting *all* of society." Brandon paused, looking somewhat apologetic. "Am I making any sense at all?"

"Well, it's not exactly the theology I learned in Catholic seminary, "but go ahead. I'm curious to see how this all ties in to your experience in Old Oberammergau."

"I'm not sure it does," Brandon admitted. "I guess I'm still searching for that rational thread. But anyway, my idea, for what it's worth, is that there really *is* a Divine Entity~call it God, or Love, or the Supreme Being, or whatever you like~who represents all Goodness. Now, separated from this Divine Entity, because of our humanity, is *another* essence or body of Spirit. And when we're born, we all inherit a tiny portion of that second body of Spirit, what we usually call our souls."

"Wait a minute, Brandon," Father Hochburg broke in. "Are you saying that our souls are something *different* from God, that they aren't the essence of the Divine Being?"

"No, I'm not saying our souls aren't divine. I'm just suggesting that they've become *separated* from the Great Divine, because we as human beings tend to be more controlled by our *human* natures than by our divine nature, that's all."

"Okay, I can see what you're getting at. Let's go on from there."

"As I see it, then, our purpose on earth is to live the best lives we can, reflected in concern for others and tolerance of their 'shortcomings'. When we die, our individual spirit reunites with the body of Spirit it came from. If we've lived a good life and learned the lessons we were supposed to, we *may* have moved that separated body of Spirit a tiny iota closer to the Supreme Being. If we haven't, we may actually have had a negative impact, as certainly a Hitler would have. But if we all keep trying, and if we slowly, gradually make the world a better place, eventually we can bring the whole body of separated Spirit back into total union with God, the Supreme Spirit. That's what I think heaven will be: a complete reintegration into Divine Love."

Brandon halted, looking down, more than a little embarrassed by the intensity with which he had expressed such a personal credo. The cleric was observing him closely, caught up in the sincerity with which the thoughts had been shared.

"Well, what do you think?" Brandon asked with a smile. "Will I be burned at the stake for heresy?"

"In Old Oberammergau, that would have been very likely," Father Hochburg told him, "but in today's world we'll give you a fair trial before we hang you." He laughed. "I'll have to admit, you've developed quite a spiritual philosophy for yourself, Brandon. I'm not saying I agree or disagree with it, but it's certainly not traditional. I do have one question, though: How does it explain what happened to you during the Passion Play?"

"That I haven't figured out completely yet," Brandon acknowledged. "It just seems to me that, by some bizarre coincidence, several members of our group *could* have 'inherited' the same bits of soul or Divine Spirit that a group of people in Old Oberammergau had years ago. I know it's stretching credulity, but I think that may be why we all had such a special sense that we'd known each other before. It's not reincarnation in the same sense that concept is usually interpreted. It's more like we all just shared a common spiritual experience." He shook his head slowly, uncertainly. Then he turned to the cleric and chuckled. "Okay, you can haul me off to the booby-hatch now."

"I don't think we can do that, Brandon," Father Hochburg replied, smiling. "I'm afraid of what you might do to the other patients." He paused, appearing to reconsider. "On the other hand, you just might cure some of them."

Despite their efforts at lightness, the two men remained sobered by what they had shared. After paying their bill, leaving a generous tip for the extra time they had occupied their table, they made their way down Dorf Strasse back to the Hotel Alte Post. Although neither expressed the thought in words, both seemed more in need of time for further private reflection rather than time for tourist pursuits.

When they reached the hotel, however, Brandon, appeared to have second thoughts. "I just remembered. I wanted to go back to the wood-carving shop and talk to the proprietor again for a few minutes before we leave town. I'll see you later, Father, at the hotel or at dinner, okay?" With that, he continued on down the thoroughfare.

The woodcarving establishment contained several customers who were examining the merchandise, exclaiming over the intricacy of the workmanship as they searched for exactly the right souvenir to take back home. Brandon made sure he was not hindering a sale before approaching the proprietor, who was still dressed in his Judas costume although this was not a scheduled Passion Play performance day.

"Ach, hello again," the proprietor greeted Brandon in recognition. "I see dot you come back, maybe for annuder Madonna, eh?" He smiled broadly, as though encountering an old friend.

Brandon laughed, "Actually, I wish I could buy *all* of your Madonnas, they're so well done. But I really wanted to ask you about something else, if you have a minute."

"Yah, yah. Most uf my customers take a long time making up dehr minds anyvay, so ve can talk." The sparkle in his eyes told Brandon that the compliment had not been missed.

"Good. Now then, I noticed from your card that your name is Schisler, is that right?"

"Yah, dot's right. Johann Schisler, dot's me." But his eyes now reflected a sudden defensiveness that Brandon didn't understand.

"Well, Mr. Schisler, what I want to ask you is this: is your family in any way related to Kaspar Schisler, the man who's supposed to have sneaked into town somehow and brought the plague to Oberammergau, many years ago?"

The proprietor recoiled as if he had been struck.

"Ach, so efen *you* know aboud dot." He was quiet for a time, then continued, "It's bad enuff ven eferyvun here in Oberammergau still blames da Schislers, but now *you*... " His voice trailed off as he looked away, deep hurt showing in his dark eyes.

Brandon immediately regretted his question. "I'm very sorry, Mr. Schisler, I honestly wasn't trying to place any blame or make you feel guilty. Please believe me. It's just that I had this strange experience during the Passion Play yesterday, like I was in a dream or something. I know it sounds crazy, but it was like I was back in Old Oberammergau at the time the plague came. Somewhere I read that a man named Kaspar Schisler brought in the plague, although nobody ever knew how he got past the guards. But he was there in my dream or trance or whatever it was. And his father was a wood-carver in a shop a lot like this one, only smaller. It's all mixed up, but still it seemed so real that I just had to come by and see if your family had any connection, historically I mean. But I'm truly very sorry my question upset you."

By now Mr. Schisler was watching Brandon intently, a strangely quizzical look having replaced the sense of injury he had displayed earlier. "How do you know aboud dat voot-carving shop?" he inquired. "How couldt you know dot?"

"I told you, I'm not sure *what* was going on, except that I felt like I was in Oberammergau back many, many years ago. In my dream I visited the shop where Kaspar's father was a wood-carver, and he made a special Madonna and Child piece that was almost exactly like the one I bought from you yesterday. It was beautiful."

A look of total amazement now emanated from the face of the shop owner. Apparently not sure how to respond to Brandon's revelation, he turned away, stammering, "Ach, chust a minute. I better vait on my customer. Yah, I be right back." With that, he moved off quickly, leaving Brandon alone, more perplexed than ever.

Having completed his sale, Mr. Schisler slowly made his way back to where Brandon was waiting. He appeared uneasy, and some of his earlier suspicious attitude seemed to have returned. As he approached, his first question was, "Vot did you say vas your name?"

"Brandon. Brandon St. Clair."

"So den, Brandon St. Clair, tell me dis: how do you know about da Madonna und Child statchues? Nobody but a Schisler knows execkly how to make dem. Nobody! So how coudt *you* possibly know, huh? How coudt you *know*?"

Now Brandon was on the defensive, and he wasn't at all sure how he should respond. "Mr. Schisler, believe me, I'm not meaning to pry or to meddle in your business or anything like that. I'm just telling you what I saw yesterday in my dream, or whatever it was that happened to me. I watched Kaspar Schisler's father carve a Madonna and Child, and that's all I can tell you. Actually, that's all I really know."

The proprietor shook his head, but now the look of distrust was replaced by a faint smile of wonderment. "In all da years, only *Schislers* know about carving da Madonna und Child," he said hesitantly. "My fodder teach me, und his fodder teach him, und so on as long as ve can remember. Alvays da Schislers haf a special vay of carving da Madonnas." Again he shook his head. "Und now you say you see it in Alte Oberammergau? I chust don't understand."

"Neither do I, Mr. Schisler. I don't understand *any* of it. I just know what I saw."

Now the proprietor was smiling broadly, as he patted Brandon on the shoulder. "Yah, yah, I belief you, Brandon. You must chust be a special fellow to know all dot." He reached to shake Brandon's hand. "I'm sorry I get angry, but ve Schislers haf been mate to feel guilty for so long, ve soon suspect *efrybody*." He paused for a moment, then added. "Dot's vun reason my son vants to get avay from da village. So he goes off to fly da planes. He say he von't be in da Play, like ve Schislers always haf been. He chust vants to fly da planes."

"You mean people still actually blame *you* for what happened so long ago?" Brandon asked, more than a little incredulous.

"Oh ya, all da time," Mr. Schisler replied with a tinge of bitterness. "Ve are still de betrayers. Vy you tink Schislers alvays play da part of Yudas?"

CHAPTER XX

The next morning, following their final breakfast at the Hotel Alte Post, the tour group assembled outside as they waited for Rudolph to bring their coach from the bus park across town. Herta was busily checking suitcases and counting tour members, making sure all was in readiness for their trip back to Munich.

As usual, the Grossfeldts were the last to arrive~mother, father, and Eloise. Alan wasn't with them. Mrs. Grossfeldt looked around anxiously, apparently trying to locate the youngster. "Have any of you seen Alan?" she inquired of the group. "He said he wanted to come down early and wait for us here. But I don't see him." She continued her worried survey.

"Has anyone seen Alan?" Herta repeated. "We need to find him right away. We can't be late, or we could miss our flight connections in Munich." Her query was met with only negative responses.

"Oh my, where could he be?" the distraught Mrs. Grossfeldt exclaimed, seemingly close to tears. "Eloise, please run back to our room, and check carefully as you go. I'll look in the dining area and the back hall. Oh my! Alan, where are you?" she called sharply, her voice manifesting her distress.

Despite some groans of frustration from the rear of the group at one more Grossfeldt delay, the tour members quickly offered to help. "Don't go too far," Herta admonished as the group spread out, "or next we'll be looking for *you*."

A frantic ten-minute search failed to locate the missing boy. Then, just as Herta was suggesting that perhaps assistance would have to be requested from the local constabulary, Brandon saw Johann Schisler emerge from his woodcarving shop. Beside him was young Alan, held firmly in the proprietor's grasp despite the boy's howls of complaint.

"There he is," Brandon announced, and all turned to watch as man and boy approached, Alan still protesting loudly while Mr. Schisler maintained his unrelenting grip.

"Ow! You're hurting me! Let go! I'll tell my dad, and then you'll be in big trouble," Alan squealed, but his cries were ignored.

When they reached the group and Mr. Schisler noticed Brandon, he smiled, nodding briefly, before asking, "Who are da parents uf dis boy?"

Mr. Grossfeldt pushed forward. "I'm his father. What's the problem here?" His tone suggested that Mr. Schisler, not Alan, had better be prepared to explain.

"I didn't do anything!" Alan whined. "I just went to his dumb old store to buy that big wooden soldier I wanted, and he grabbed me and started hurting me. It's all his fault!"

"Alan! You know you couldn't buy that soldier," Mrs. Grossfeldt interrupted. "You don't have any money."

Mr. Schisler had not yet relaxed his hold on Alan. Now he addressed the Grossfeldts, giving no indication whatsoever of being intimidated. "Yah, he come to my shop, und he say he vants to buy dot bik vooden soldier I haf. Den ven he vants to pay for it, he gifs me dis." Mr. Schisler held out a Visa credit card, obviously issued to Mr. Grossfeldt. "I tell him I tink he's chust a liddle young, und dot's ven he start calling me bad names, und so I take hold on him und come looking for you. You see?"

The Grossfeldt parents looked first at one another, then at Alan, as they realized what must have happened. Mr. Schisler released the youngster and stepped back.

Recompense

∞

"How did you get my credit card, Alan?" Mr. Grossfeldt demanded seizing the boy by both arms. "Answer me!"

"Ow! Now you're hurting me, too! Quit it! I didn't do anything," Alan whimpered, sensing that he may have over-stepped even the loose boundaries set by his parents.

"How did you get my card?" his father repeated, his voice rising.

Seeing there was no escape, Alan turned defiant. "Well, I told you I wanted the *big* wooden soldier, not that dumb little one. Why didn't you buy it for me when I asked for it? It's your fault! That's why I had to take your dumb old credit card when you weren't looking. Big deal!"

"Alan, you're so stupid!" Eloise broke in. "You should know you can't buy stuff with Dad's credit card."

"Make her shut up, Mama," Alan whined. "Why is everybody mad at me, anyway? Why aren't you mad at that mean store man instead? He's the one who hurt my arm. Make him go to jail, okay, Mama? Okay?"

Alan eyed the assembled group, seeking sympathy for his plight, but he found none. Even his usually indulgent parents showed their exasperation. His father hauled him unceremoniously toward the waiting bus with the stern warning, "You'd better get on that bus this instant, young man. We'll deal with you later."

Eloise, seeing her opportunity, squeezed up next to Alan and pinched him as hard as she could, leading to further loud protests. "Ow! Mama, Eloise pinched me! She did it on purpose, too!"

"Eloise! I'm surprised at you!"

"He's lying, Mom, just 'cuz he's in trouble."

"Why's everybody being so mean to me? I didn't do anything!" Still complaining, Alan disappeared into the bus.

With everyone finally ready to go, Herta and Rudolph consulted briefly regarding the quickest way to return to Munich, considering their reduced time schedule. They settled on the most direct route, though it meant taking a less-traveled road for a portion of the journey.

Then, as the tourists bade their last farewells to the charming little village that had brought such dramatic experiences to their lives, Rudolph maneuvered the bus expertly down the narrow street to the main road, which would connect them with the motorway.

As they proceeded, Herta alerted the tour members to watch for a complex of buildings on their left. This, she told them, would be Ettal Abbey, a huge Benedictine monastery that dated back to 1330 but which had been "modernized" into Gothic architectural style in the 18th Century.

"It really needs to be viewed from the hill above because of the high walls," Herta told them, "but unfortunately, there's no road up there."

Instead, since their timetable didn't permit a visit, Rudolph pulled the bus off into the parking area nearby long enough to allow photographs of the impressive edifice. Margaret Wilson seemed especially appreciative. "Thank you so much, Rudolph," she said as she returned to the bus. "That was very thoughtful."

To the south, as they continued on through the switchbacks, Brandon got his last good look at the Bavarian Alps. Far to the right, Herta pointed out the Zugspitze, Germany's tallest mountain, locale for many of the winter sports activities in the region. Brandon nodded in parting, not certain if he would ever view the landmark again.

Soon Rudolph turned off onto a narrow but well-maintained road that took them down from the Alpine foothills to more typical Bavarian terrain. A short distance farther on, he turned off once more, this time onto a motorway that enabled them to make excellent time as they sped past Lake Starnberg and on to Munich.

They made their connections for the flight from Munich to Frankfurt without serious problems. The only misgivings came from the realization that their mutual adventure was now near its conclusion. Also, there were several nostalgic moments as they said good-bye to their skilled bus driver, Rudolph, who had done everything he could to make their journey as pleasant as possible. Appreciation was reflected in the tip envelopes slipped covertly to Rudolph as the travelers said their farewells.

At Frankfurt, Herta performed her last official duties as tour director, assisting the group in collecting their luggage, escorting them through the stringent security check, and finally depositing them at the proper gate for their flight home. Here again, sincere expressions of gratitude and affection accompanied their parting. Brandon was amazed at how close-knit the members of the group had become, almost like family, in the course of their associated travels.

Now all that remained was to wait for the boarding call that would launch the travelers on their long journey home. As they passed the time in personal exchanges and reminiscences, a note of sadness was evident beneath the excitement surrounding their return. They knew they had come to the end of a unique experience in their lives.

As they moved at last toward the ramp leading to their Lufthansa 747, they did so with good-natured camaraderie~except for Alan Grossfeldt, who insisted that he be at the head of the line. By now, however, the remaining tour members had become indulgent enough to let him have his way, since they knew they would not have to listen to his peevish demands much longer.

Brandon followed Father Hochburg briskly down the ramp, his small carry-on case and topcoat securely in hand, paying little attention to their surroundings as they chatted in their usual amicable manner. He knew these would be among their last opportunities to exchange ideas before they went their separate ways in Boston, and he had grown genuinely fond of the genial priest.

Then he saw her.

She was standing just inside the doorway of the plane, greeting passengers and directing them toward their seats, part of her duties as Head Flight Attendant. Her entire demeanor exuded an inner energy, a caring concern, a vitality that was both singular and extraordinary. Golden blonde hair framed a face of exceptional beauty, soft and delicate with a glow that matched the radiance of her smile.

Brandon could only stare, transfixed. Never had he seen a woman he considered more beautiful, more natural in manner, than this "vision" before him. He failed to realize that at sight of her he had stopped absolutely still, until Mrs. Scheer, following behind, coughed politely and asked, "Is something wrong, Brandon?"

"No, uh, not at all," he stammered as he moved forward, color rising in his cheeks. Still he could not bring himself to look away, and so it was that when his turn came to be greeted by the alluring Attendant, Brandon found himself gazing directly into a pair of eyes so blue, so deep that his discomfiture was multiplied.

To his complete surprise, those eyes now reflected a sudden flash of recognition, and a look of wonderment crossed the exquisite face. The full lips parted, mouthing a soft, questioning "Rolf?" Then puzzlement supplanted recognition in the depths of blue, and she looked away quickly, her embarrassment equaling Brandon's. In that moment, Brandon noticed for the first time the name on her identification badge below her title: "Head Flight Attendant"~"Inga."

Totally unnerved by what had taken place, Brandon glanced back at Mrs. Scheer, who favored him with a knowing smile that only heightened his confusion. It was all too much. He turned and strode hurriedly down the aisle, eager to find his seat so that he could relax and sort things out.

Locating his assigned spot, he saw that fortune had been with him once more~it was an aisle seat next to Father Hochburg, which would enable the two to extend their cordial relationship a little longer. The priest had missed out on the exchange between Brandon and the Flight Attendant, but he was quick to note that something had definitely upset the younger man's customary equilibrium.

Recompense

∞

"So, Brandon, it looks like we're stuck with each other a little longer." He chuckled. "Or are you planning to take off on another one of your mystical journeys? You seem a bit flustered. Did something happen to upset you?"

Brandon sank back and drew a deep breath before answering. Then he turned to the cleric, attempting a casual smile. "I sure wouldn't want to have anything on my conscience if I attended your church, Father. You don't miss a thing, do you? You have a real knack for 'reading' people."

"It goes with the territory, Brandon. Now, don't try any more of your evasive 'lawyer talk' to get out of telling me what happened, okay?"

By now Brandon was feeling somewhat more settled, but he wasn't sure he wanted to share this latest unexplainable experience just yet. "Give me a few minutes, please, will you, Father? It's another one of those things I don't have an answer for, but at least this one does seem to have more positive possibilities." As he finished, Brandon was smiling broadly.

"Oh, ho! Do I detect some vague elements of intrigue here, or has our reserved bachelor just met his Waterloo?"

The remark caught Brandon off guard, but he recovered quickly. "Like I said, Father, you have an incredible insight into human nature. But you're still going to have to wait awhile before I tell you anything." With that, he smiled and closed his eyes.

His escape was short-lived. With all of the passengers loaded and Lufthansa Flight 1247 ready for take-off, Brandon heard a Flight Attendant moving down the aisle, giving last minute assistance or instruction as needed: "May I help you with your seat belt, ma'am?" "I'm sorry, sir, but you'll have to bring your seat completely upright for take-off." There could be no mistaking that rich, melodious voice. It had to be Inga.

Brandon opened his eyes and watched her approaching, mesmerized once more by her beauty and the grace of her movements. When she reached his row, she hesitated briefly. A look of pleasure high-lighted the blue of her eyes, accompanied by a tinge of continuing embarrassment. But the luminous smile that had captivated Brandon earlier returned as she said softly, "I'm sorry about that mix-up out there. I thought you were someone I once knew."

"No problem at all. I'm afraid I reacted rather strangely myself." He mirrored her smile. Then she was gone, leaving him with a puzzling new thought to ponder.

Father Hochburg had been an interested but silent observer. Now, giving Brandon a perceptive wink, he grinned. "Well, I don't think you'll have to explain anything to me after all." With a chuckle, he settled back for take-off.

Flustered anew, Brandon was happy for the bustle of activity accompanying their departure, since it enabled him to avoid a response. He stretched his legs, then sat quietly as the pilot taxied their plane to the assigned runway. After a brief wait for clearance, the jet made a smooth lift-off that marked the beginning of their eight-hour journey back to Boston. The flight pattern, they were told, would take them along the most direct route over the waters of the North Atlantic.

Flight 1247 settled into its routine, with Inga and her courteous crew serving drinks and snacks while passengers adjusted to the constrictions dictated by their new environment. A generally happy mood, evidenced by light-hearted banter, pervaded their section of the airplane, perhaps based on anticipation of reunion with loved ones or adventures yet to be experienced.

Following a rather lengthy, animated conversation with Father Hochburg, Brandon excused himself to move around and stretch a bit. As he worked his way slowly down the aisle, he spotted Inga seated at the Flight Attendant's station, busy with paperwork. She looked up as he neared, her warm smile a signal of welcome.

"Hi, my name is Brandon St. Clair," he began uncertainly, not sure how to broach the real subject he hoped to pursue. He paused, clearing his throat before proceeding. "What I was wondering is, where do you think we might have met before?"

Inga glanced down, and again a slight blush heightened the elegant charm of her face. "You just reminded me of someone from a long, long time ago," she replied quietly, her eyes meeting his. "Like I said, I'm really sorry."

"But I'm intrigued, I really am. I've been trying to figure out where I could have seen you before. Where is it that you're from?"

"Oh, from a little town in southern Bavaria, one you've probably never even heard of. It's called Oberammergau."

"Oberammergau?" Brandon repeated. "What a surprise! You're not going to believe this, but I was just there."

"You were in Oberammergau?"

"Yes, I was, just a short time ago. In fact, quite a few of your passengers were in my tour group and we attended a performance of the Passion Play. I can't believe you actually live there."

"Oh, but I do. It's wonderful that you saw our Play. We're so proud of what it stands for. Except for the years when we put on the Play, though, I'm afraid tourists pretty much ignore us."

"But your town is such a unique place, even without the Play. You have your beautiful church, the little shops, the special artwork on your houses, all of it. My friend Father Hochburg and I even visited your cemetery."

"You went to our cemetery? Why would you want to go there, if I may ask?"

"We both wanted to see if we could locate any of the graves of people who died from the plague back in the 1600's, when the 'Black Death' threatened to decimate your village." Brandon paused, feeling a bit foolish. "Do I take it you don't think that was such a great idea?"

"Oh, no, Brandon, just the opposite! The cemetery has always been one of my favorite spots in Oberammergau. I used to spend hours there when I was a little girl, imagining what it must have been like during the plague, and how frightened the people must have been and everything. After all, those poor people are why we have our wonderful Passion Play now, and we should never forget them." Inga halted, then added somewhat apologetically, "I hope that doesn't sound too morbid."

Brandon's smile almost matched her own. "Not to me, it doesn't. Would you believe that's exactly why Father Hochburg and I hoped to find those graves? We felt that the human tragedy could easily get lost in all of the pageantry, so we wanted to remember the people more as real living individuals, just like us."

"That's truly remarkable, Brandon." He felt a thrill at the way she repeated his name, almost as though it was an intimate caress. There was no question that he was falling hopelessly under her spell.

"By the way," Inga continued, "did you know that our pilot is from Oberammergau too? I know that must sound like a really strange coincidence, but it's true. We've worked together many times over the years."

"Are you serious?"

"Absolutely!"

"That does seem almost too much to be believable, considering the size of your town. But I can certainly see why he'd like working with you, Inga."

She smiled at the compliment. "Would you like to meet him?"

"Yes, I would, very much."

"He usually comes through this section at some time during the flight to chat with the passengers. I'll introduce you, if I'm here at the time. But I'm afraid he doesn't feel quite like you do about our home town, for some reason. His name is Schisler, Captain Kaspar Schisler."

CHAPTER XXI

Why he should feel such a resurgence of foreboding at Inga's disclosure Brandon wasn't sure. Intellectually, he knew his apprehensions were irrational. After all, what sinister connection could there be between a man who had lived in an isolated Alpine village more than three centuries before and the pilot of a modern-day airliner making a routine flight across the Atlantic, simply because both had been given the same name? What harm could possibly come from that? Yet, as he thought of the bizarre experiences, the unexplainable coincidences that had been part of the past weeks, he knew that nothing seemed any longer to be beyond the realm of possibility.

Returning to his seat, Brandon decided not to mention what he had learned to Father Hochburg, who was now deeply engrossed in the book he was reading. Instead, he did a quick mental summation, courtroom style, of the series of improbable happenings during the past days, reaching no new conclusions. The events still defied plausible explanation.

Sure enough, just as Inga had indicated, the pilot entered their section of the airplane, greeting passengers and chatting as he moved down the aisle. When he reached Brandon's seat, he extended his hand and pronounced with a friendly smile, "You must be Brandon St. Clair. Inga told me where to find you."

Brandon returned the pilot's firm handshake. "It's nice to meet you, Captain Schisler. This is Father Hochburg," he added, indicating the priest. "I understand you're from Oberammergau."

"Yes, that's right. Inga tells me that some of you attended the Passion Play there recently."

"We did, and it was a wonderful experience," Father Hochburg broke in. "It's something I've dreamed about seeing for years, and I certainly wasn't disappointed."

"Even five and a half hours of German couldn't discourage us," Brandon laughed. Then he turned serious. "Tell me if I'm right, please: your father played the role of Judas in the play, didn't he?"

The same look of guarded suspicion that Brandon had encountered in the woodcarving shop clouded the pilot's face. "How did you know he was my father? Who told you that?"

Brandon realized that he had again touched a nerve. "Please understand, Captain Schisler, he did a wonderful job of acting, very natural for the part. I ran into him later in his woodcarving shop, and we got to talking, and that's when he told me his son was a pilot. I guess I just put two and two together. After all, how many Captain Schislers from Oberammergau can there be?" Brandon smiled broadly, trying to emphasize that no offense had been intended.

The Captain appeared to relax. "It seems to be just one of those 'small world' things, doesn't it?" He still looked puzzled, however. "But what brought me into the conversation, anyway? Usually all Dad wants to talk about is his carvings."

"Well, I bought one of those special Madonna and Child pieces he does, the ones that are so unique. He told me how the carving secret had been passed on from generation to generation of Schislers, but that his son preferred flying airplanes to learning woodcarving secrets. That's pretty much all there was to it."

By now Captain Schisler was smiling again. "Yes, that sounds like Dad, all right. He really takes pride in those pieces, and I know he'd like me to work with him, and someday maybe even play the role of…." His voice trailed off, as he finished half to himself, "Who knows? Maybe someday...." He hunched his shoulders, then waved a genial goodbye and moved on.

When the pilot was out of earshot, Father Hochburg turned to Brandon. "Well, that was revealing, wasn't it? So our pilot really is a Schisler, just like the Schislers you ran into in your strange experience in Old Oberammergau?"

"The same. And his name isn't just Schisler, it's Captain *Kaspar* Schisler."

"Whoa!"

"It's true! The Flight Attendant told me when we chatted earlier."

"Talk about weird coincidences! You're beginning to scare me, Brandon, with all of these spooky things going on around you that don't seem to have any rational explanation."

Brandon attempted to appear casual, though he felt his strange sense of unease returning even more forcefully. "What really scares *me*, Father, is that we've all put our lives in the hands of another Kaspar Schisler. You know what happened last time." He laughed, but the laugh lacked sincerity.

In an effort to lift the gloomy mood that had descended, Brandon again excused himself to move around their section of the plane. He had not had many opportunities recently to visit with Herman Meyer, so he now sought out the stocky little man seated far toward the rear.

"How's it going, Herman?" Brandon greeted his traveling comrade. "Are you glad we're getting closer to home?"

"Ach, yah, but also a little sorry the trip has to be over with. I'm afraid I won't be seeing again the good people who have become my new friends."

"I think most of us feel that way. But who knows, maybe we'll run into each other again. You're from the Bay Area, aren't you?"

"Yah, from Richmond."

"Well, that's not very far from the City. I think I told you that I live in San Francisco, didn't I?" Brandon took a business card from his wallet and handed it to Herman. "My phone number's on here. Call me any-time you like, Herman."

"Ach, I'd like that very much, Brandon, if you tink you might want to hear from an old refinery worker."

"Is that what you do, work in one of those oil refineries in Richmond?"

"Yah, that's how I make my living." Herman paused, and a sly smile crept across his face. "But what I really like to call myself is an artist." Again he hesitated, chuckling. "I guess I don't look much like one though, huh?"

"An artist? Why, that's great, Herman. What kind of art work do you do?"

"In my spare time, I do metal sculpturing," Herman announced rather proudly. "Big ones, little ones, all kinds. I just like to work with all sorts of metal."

"I'm impressed! Do you have a studio?"

"Nah, I chust work at home, in my back yard mostly." Herman laughed. "You should see that back yard, Brandon. Pretty soon there's no room for anything else, it's so full of my sculptures."

"I'd really like to see that. In fact, there's nothing I'd like better than to buy one of those pieces for myself. My back yard isn't very big, but I know just the spot for one of your smaller sculptures. How about it?"

Herman's heavy features crinkled into a broad, happy smile, his eyes bright with pleasure and pride. Softly he replied, "I'd be honored, Brandon. I truly would."

"That's just great! Give me a call and I'll come make my selection as soon as we can arrange it."

Herman remained silent for a moment, looking down, before he raised his thoughtful, honest gaze. "Would it be all right with you if I make a new sculpture, chust for you? A special one?"

"Why, yes, of course it would! Do you have something specific in mind?"

Recompense

"Well, I was tinking. Remember that statue of Jesus on the donkey in front of the theater at Oberammergau? You know, the one standing on the rock with the water coming out?"

"Sure! I found it really intriguing, especially trying to figure out its meaning."

"Yah, that's how I felt, too. So, what if I try to make you a small copy of it for your garden? Then you could spend the rest of your life figuring it out." Herman laughed heartily at his own jest.

"What a great idea, Herman! I'd love it, I really would! It would be a fantastic reminder of this whole trip, and especially of you."

The beaming face, the look of pride on Herman's face led Brandon to pose a further question that he had been pondering. "May I ask you one more thing, Herman? When you mentioned the Oberammergau statue, it reminded me of something." Brandon halted briefly, not wanting to break the congenial spirit of the moment. "Why do you suppose we both felt so much like we already knew each other when we first met? Do you have any kind of explanation?"

Now Herman turned serious. "I wondered a lot about that, Brandon. I tried and tried to tink what could be the reason, but I chust don't know." He shook his head slowly, keeping his eyes focused intently on Brandon. Then he relaxed and his customary good nature returned, along with his cordial smile. "Who knows, maybe we're chust kindred spirits, that's all," he finished with a chuckle.

Brandon didn't push the issue. "You're probably right, Herman. Maybe we were related in our last life, or something like that." He laughed along with Herman. "Anyway, I'm certainly looking forward to my new work of art." Clapping Herman on the shoulder, he ambled back down the aisle toward his own seat.

Earlier, Brandon had noticed Louise Scheer as she took her seat several rows ahead of his own. Now he made his way forward to chat with her, hoping to reinforce his association with the pleasant woman before they parted. To his surprise, he found Margaret Wilson also seated in the same row. This would enable him to say his farewells to both women.

"Well, well, it's nice to find the two of you together," he began.

"Why hello, Brandon. It's nice to see you, too."

"Have you two been reminiscing about our tour, or are you already planning your next adventure?"

Mrs. Scheer responded in her usual warm manner. "Oh, we've been talking about a great many things, including you." She laughed at Brandon's look of surprise, then quickly changed the subject. "Margaret's been telling me how she has to go back to work at Shelbourne Museum, and I've been telling her she needs to come out to Mendocino to try some of my baked goods." She laughed again.

"Louise says she thinks you might have been to her Bake Shoppe, trying some of her macadamia nut cookies," Margaret added.

"Yes, we tried to figure out where we had met before and decided that it must have been at her shop." The thought took him back momentarily to his reverie in Oberammergau, but he went on, "You'd love Mendocino, Margaret. It's such a quaint little town."

"That's what Louise insists, too. Maybe I can vacation out on the West Coast sometime and check it out for myself. In the meantime, I fear that 'duty calls' and I'll have to get back to the museum."

With a smile, Brandon returned to something Mrs. Scheer had mentioned. "By the way, I'm curious as to just how I got into your conversation, except I'm almost afraid to ask."

Margaret lowered her gaze, a faint blush rising in her cheeks. Mrs. Scheer, however, was happy to explain. "Oh, I was telling Margaret that, when our tour first began, I really thought the two of you might get together somehow. You'd make a fine-looking couple. But now I see that someone else has caught your eye."

Recompense

∽

She laughed softly, approval reflecting from her kind blue eyes. Then she turned to Margaret, giving her arm an affectionate pat. "I'm sorry if I've embarrassed you, my dear."

Now it was Brandon who felt the warmth rise in his face at the obvious reference to Inga. To cover his uneasiness, he laughed lightly. "You're as bad as Father Hochburg. Neither of you two miss a thing, do you?"

Mrs. Scheer smiled pleasantly. "She looks like a very nice young woman, Brandon~so attractive and vibrant." For a moment, a wistful look crowded out the smile. "In fact, she's exactly the kind of person I'd have wanted for a daughter."

Once more, Brandon's eyes widened in astonishment. Disconcerted, he could only stammer, "I, uh, guess I'd better get back to my seat now. It was nice chatting with you both."

As he turned to go, he noted the distinctive aroma of fresh-baked cookies wafting gently through the air.

Father Hochburg was napping. Slipping quietly into his seat, careful not to wake his resting seatmate, Brandon relaxed and enjoyed the peaceful moments. Mrs. Grossfeldt, seated across the aisle from him, looked over and smiled, then turned her attention back to the children. The Grossfeldt's still remained an enigma, and Brandon wondered if anyone could ever really break through the wall by which they separated themselves from others.

His thoughts transferred abruptly into more pleasant channels when he saw Inga emerge from the First Class section and come down the aisle toward him. Despite Brandon's best efforts to maintain a detached outward composure, he felt his pulse quicken with a sense of expectancy. Sure enough, she paused at his row, her radiant smile accompanied by a soft, "Hi, Brandon."

Checking to see that Father Hochburg was still asleep, Brandon whispered, "Can I meet you back at your station? Maybe we can talk. I don't want to wake him up."

Inga nodded and led the way. She settled into her Attendants' seat, indicating a spot near by for Brandon. The expressive blue eyes mirrored both happiness and curiosity as she asked, "Is there a problem?"

"Oh no, not at all. It's been a great flight." He hesitated for an instant. "I'm just sorry it's almost over."

Inga's graceful eyebrows arched. "Oh? That's kind of unusual. Mostly, our passengers are anxious to get to where they're going."

"It isn't that I'm not anxious to get back home." Another hesitant pause followed. "It's just that when we get to Boston I'll be changing airlines and going on to San Francisco~and you *won't* be." He felt himself flush slightly as he finished, uncertain of what her response would be.

He need not have been concerned. The look of deep pleasure, as well as the enchanting smile, informed Brandon that the feelings were reciprocal. "How sweet of you Brandon. I'll have to admit I've had the same thoughts. I'm not sure what it is, but it just seems that we still have a lot to tell each other."

Brandon was ecstatic. "I'm so glad you feel that way, Inga. Who knows, if we had enough time, I might even tell you about my really strange experience during the Passion Play performance. Maybe *you'd* have an explanation. I certainly don't."

"Now you've got me curious! We'll just have to figure something out." She was silent for a bit, thinking, then inquired, "Do you *have* to go right back to San Francisco, Brandon? Is there some way you could extend your vacation in Boston for a few days?"

"Well, I don't really have to be back at any certain time, but my flight's all arranged and I'm afraid I always like to do everything according to plan." He grinned. "I guess it's the lawyer in me, trying to stay organized."

"Do you think you could break your pattern a bit? I could try to help."

"How's that?"

Recompense

∽

"Well, I know quite a few people from the other airlines. Maybe I could find someone to change your ticket, to reschedule your flight for a later date. I'll have a few days off between flights myself."

Brandon recognized his dilemma. Any "spur of the moment" change in plans was contrary to his entire *modus operandi*. Yet, to make the change would enable him to spend time with the one woman he found more alluring than any he could remember. It was an intriguing temptation.

"It's up to you, Brandon." Her eyes, the welcome in her voice, everything told him what she hoped the answer would be.

Brandon hesitated, torn between his natural reticence to alter an orderly, established course of action and the proffered opportunity to spend more time with this enticing young woman whom he found so irresistible.

Then he broke into a wide grin. His heart had won the struggle with his head.

"Inga, that's an offer I truly can't refuse. For once in my life, I'd rather change my plans than have everything be so predictable~and especially when I consider the benefits!"

"I'm very glad you feel that way, Brandon. I'll make the necessary contacts as soon as we land, if that's all right with you."

"Absolutely! The extra time should give us a chance to talk, to get to know each other better. There are so many things that I want to tell you, especially about the unbelievable stuff that happened to me in Oberammergau." His look was a combination of pleasure and awe. "I don't usually change my itinerary like this, but I feel really good about it."

Inga reached out, placing her soft hand warmly on his, happiness radiating from the depths of her azure eyes. "I'm so pleased you decided to stay in Boston, Brandon. I can't tell you how much. We can make the ticket changes, I'm certain…. *if* you don't change your mind first." She finished with a laugh that held both joy and concern.

"Not a chance! I can't stay in my 'tried and true' security mode forever, can I?" He looked deep into those remarkable eyes and gently squeezed her hand. "I really wouldn't miss this opportunity for anything!"

Her look of delight only added to Brandon's sense of self-satisfaction at having broken from his usual patterned existence. As she rose, still smiling warmly, he stood as well, not yet ready to relinquish the touch of her hand. She leaned against his shoulder affectionately, hesitant to go, and he felt a surge of tender emotion unlike anything he could remember.

At last she said quietly, "I see Captain Schisler has just turned on the 'Fasten Seat Belt' sign again. I'll have to go now and make sure everything's secure. The latest weather update we received suggests that what's up ahead of us might not be too encouraging."

"Oh?"

"Yes, the report indicated a good-sized storm between us and Boston, and our radar shows it's pretty serious."

"What does that mean for our flight?"

"Well, we can either go around it, which would mean we'll be late getting into Boston, or we can take a chance and try to fly straight through it. It's up to the Captain to make an 'informed decision' in a case like this."

"What do you think he'll do?"

"Captain Schisler is extremely proud of his 'on time' record. He hates running late, or altering his set course. He's a little like you, I think, when it comes to wanting to do things according to schedule." She smiled, her eyes glowing softly at the comparison. "Unlike you, as long as I've known him, he's never changed his plans." She turned to move down the aisle, adding, "Now we'll just have to hope he makes the right decision."

CHAPTER XXII

The first indication that all was not well came when Captain Schisler's crisp voice echoed over the intercom: "Ladies and gentlemen, this is your Captain speaking. Please return to your seats, and make sure your seat belts are fastened securely. We expect to encounter some heavy turbulence shortly. As a precautionary measure, I have asked that Flight Attendants be seated as well." His voice was steady, reassuring, giving no hint of possible disaster. Good-natured chatter continued throughout the cabin as passengers settled down to comply with the Captain's request.

The impact of the storm's fiendish power was as sudden as it was unexpected. Like a drifting leaf caught in a passing whirlwind, Lufthansa Flight 1247 was buffeted by the frightening force of a blast that had appeared as only a threatening disturbance on the aircraft's radar. Now the danger was real, inescapable. The jet floundered under the fury of the gale, shuddering, then dropping erratically in altitude as a wave of panic radiated through the cabin.

Brandon watched helplessly as his fellow travelers reeled under the onslaught. Cries of fright melded with the clamor of unsecured objects sent flying by the abruptness of the descent. An electronic game-board with which Alan Grossfeldt had been playing arced through the air, bounced harmlessly off a nearby seatback, then clattered noisily down the aisle. Alan's frantic cries of, "Gimme my game-board back!" helped to swell the general uproar.

Once more the Captain's resolute voice broke through the din: "Ladies and gentlemen, we apologize for the inconvenience created by this intense weather. Rest assured the airplane is in no immediate danger, and we will continue on course. At the same time, I am requesting permission from Air Traffic Control for descent to a lower altitude in hopes of finding a smoother flying level. Hopefully, that will enable us to get safely through this turbulence. For now, please stay in your seats with your seat belts securely fastened. Thank you."

In spite of the plane's continuing tremors, Captain Schisler's calm words served to help ease the tension for the passengers. The hubbub of sound gradually lessened as Flight Attendants were able to leave their seats to check for possible problems. Though badly shaken, no one seemed to be injured, and the anxious travelers gradually began to relax.

The turmoil did permit Brandon to observe Inga in action. She appeared to be everywhere, with a smile here, a pat on the shoulder there, with words of encouragement to both her crew and clients. He noted that her inspirational reassurances extended to everyone, but were especially comforting to the children.

As she passed Brandon's seat, she reached down to squeeze his hand, the look in her eyes reflecting her obvious affection. The action was not lost on Father Hochburg. "She's a real gem, isn't she, Brandon? And I don't think you'll have to worry about getting your share of attention for the rest of this flight." He settled back and chuckled knowingly.

For once Brandon did not try to deflect the implication. "Yes, she really is something special, Father. In fact, if this plane makes it to Boston in one piece, we're hoping to rearrange my schedule so that we can spend some extra time there getting better acquainted."

"Well, well, isn't that interesting? But why am I not surprised?" The priest beamed approvingly. "Who knows, if you happen to have any spare time left over, you and I might be able to get together again, too." He gave Brandon's arm a friendly squeeze. "And I don't think you need to worry about making it to Boston. I have a hunch we'll get there even if you have to get out and personally carry this airplane!"

Brandon laughed. "I hope you're right~about everything except me carrying the plane, that is. Anyway, I'm ready for us to get through all of this turbulence, aren't you? It's making me a bit woozy."

A deafening, cataclysmic clap of thunder reverberated through the plane, leaving no doubt that nature's upheaval had not yet run its course. The jet shook violently, as the cabin lights flickered. Cries of fright mingled with startled exclamations: "Oh, my God!" "What was *that*?" "What's happening?"

Still, the clamor proved to be only a harbinger of the real disaster to come. Without further warning, a second crash of thunder, more terrifying and ferocious than the first, engulfed the airplane. The savage crescendo was accompanied by a flash so brilliant that it illuminated the entire area in a phosphorescent glow. The jet tossed like a twig caught in a wild sea, rocking, quivering as though ready to disintegrate. To add to the horror, the entire plane was plunged into absolute darkness.

Screams of alarm pierced the black gloom as pandemonium reigned. Continuing drastic convulsions of the airplane furthered the aura of doom. Above the din, Brandon could hear Father Hochburg repeating in somber tones, "Hail Mary, full of grace, blessed art Thou among women...."

As the cacophony continued, a thought flashed implausibly through Brandon's mind: This was the same type of panicked reaction citizens of Oberammergau had exhibited during his reverie, when they faced the threat of death from the Black Plague. Why did one's imminent demise always seem so frightening, he wondered? Didn't most people profess to believe in a life after death, in a place of unmatched beauty called Heaven? Then why were we all so reluctant to go there when the time actually came for the transition? Somewhere in human nature there appeared to lurk a fierce determination to cling to life as tenaciously as possible for as long as possible. Was this a contradiction? Or was it only further evidence of humanity's spiritual separation from the Divine?

By now, the acrid smell of smoke had begun to permeate the cabin, lending an additional element to the atmosphere of catastrophe. Leaning toward Father Hochburg, Brandon whispered, "Do you smell that? Could the plane be on fire?"

The priest sniffed and looked around. "I can't see anything that looks like flames. But it does seem to be getting awfully stuffy in here. I wonder what's going on."

"It doesn't smell like regular smoke to me. It's more like an odor I remember when I accidentally shorted out my coffeepot and blew a whole circuit. It's something electrical, I think."

As suddenly as they had gone out, the cabin lights flashed back on~dim at first, then glimmering to full brightness. Cries of "Yeah!" and "Thank God!" welcomed the reprieve, as passengers peered about anxiously to assess the situation. The plane still wobbled unsteadily, but somehow everything seemed less ominous once the darkness had been dispelled.

The Captain's voice crackled over the intercom: "Ladies and gentlemen, it appears our plane suffered a lightning strike to the pod of the right inboard engine. This caused a temporary loss of electrical power, but we have managed to restore the system."

Mr. Grossfeldt's voice rang out over that of the pilot: "My God, man, what are you saying? A lightening strike? We're not going to make it, are we?"

"There is no immediate cause for alarm," Captain Schisler went on. "Our remaining three engines are all working well, and fortunately there was no fire. However, we have experienced a loss of pressurization, and are still completing a procedural checklist of our system. We hope to maintain our current flying altitude of 42,000 feet, if the problem can be resolved. If not, we will be forced to reduce altitude to a much lower elevation as quickly as possible. Please keep your seatbelts fastened and, should they deploy, be prepared to use your oxygen masks."

Passengers looked around at their neighbors, uneasy, uncertain as to what might be in store. Brandon heard Mrs. Grossfeldt trying to calm her husband, "It's all right, dear. If they could fix the lights, they can probably fix the pressure thing, too."

Her optimism proved to be unfounded.

In minutes, the airplane began nosing sharply downward, without warning or announcement. The Captain's worst fears had obviously become reality, and a headlong emergency descent had been initiated.

A new wave of panic surged through the airplane. Despite the earlier words of reassurance, basic fright again became the operative emotion as travelers were subjected to one more unanticipated emergency. A babble of intermingled wails, prayers, and moans filled the air.

Their descent was both precipitous and unnerving. For minutes that seemed like an eternity, the jet plummeted earthward, groaning and shuddering under the gravitational strain. Brandon swallowed hard to relieve the pressure in his ears. Across the aisle, Mr. Grossfeldt grumbled, complaining loudly enough for everyone to hear, "What's the matter with these people? Why won't anybody tell us what's happening?" Passengers clung desperately to their vibrating seats, too terrified to protest or cry out. Father Hochburg resumed his litany: "Hail, Mary, full of grace…."

Just as it seemed that plane and passengers had reached the apex of their endurance, the Captain came on the intercom: "Ladies and gentlemen, we apologize for the discomfort caused by our speedy descent, but it was made necessary by our unresolved pressurization problem. The Second Officer and I are completing our rapid depressurization checklist, while the First Officer has deployed the speedbrakes and will continue bringing the aircraft down at the rate of approximately 6,000 feet per minute until we reach an altitude of 10,000 feet. So far, all systems are holding."

A moment of quiet followed, and Brandon tried to imagine the intensity of activity that must be occurring in the cockpit as the three Flight Officers tried to cope with the emergency. He glanced around to the Attendant's station. There was Inga, clearly concerned, alertly observing reactions to the crisis. For an instant their eyes met, enabling Brandon to convey a glimmer of his deeply-felt feelings for her.

Then the Captain's announcement resumed: "We are now approaching 15,000 feet. "In a few seconds, your oxygen masks will be dropping. Please put them on carefully, as you were instructed. As I said, we will need to continue our descent until we reach 10,000 feet. Please try to remain calm."

As if to validate the pilot's words, a bouncing profusion of oxygen masks dropped from compartments above the passengers. Brandon could understand why, as he had been told, Flight Attendants referred to the aftermath as a "rubber jungle." Surprise and uncertainty regarding proper usage added to the spectacle of confusion.

"Now, let's see if I can remember how this thing is supposed to go on," Father Hochburg mumbled as he examined the elastic straps of his mask.

"Here, let me give you a hand." Brandon's voice was muffled by his own mask, already secured. He could feel the refreshing surge of oxygen flowing into his lungs. Soon both men sat back, breathing easily.

Across the aisle, things were not working out as smoothly for the Grossfeldt family. Alan and his parents had their masks in place, but Eloise was still struggling with hers, becoming more and more agitated. Somehow the air tube on her mask had become tangled. "Mom, Dad, help me!" she wailed. "I can't make this dumb thing work! I can't breathe! Help me!"

Recompense

The more she twisted the mask, the worse the muddle became, and the louder she screamed. Both Mr. and Mrs. Grossfeldt reached over the seat, trying frantically to help, but only managed to make the tangle worse.

"Somebody help me! I can't get any air! I'm going to die!" Eloise had given way to total panic.

Brandon released his seat belt and pulled off his mask. He tried to move across the aisle to give assistance, but the aircraft's sudden dip threw him back against his seat. Down the aisle, he saw Inga also attempting to move forward, despite the order that Flight Attendants remain seated during the emergency. She had donned her portable oxygen mask, but she too was unable to make progress against the plane's gyrations.

Above everything sounded Eloise's gasps for air and her terrified, breathless plea: "Help me, somebody! I'm going to die! Please help me! Pleeease!"

CHAPTER XXIII

In this crisis, aid for Eloise came from the least expected quarter. Alan Grossfeldt, sensing his sister's fright, took a deep breath of oxygen from his mask, then removed the elastic strap encircling his head. "Here, Eloise, try mine." He held the mask to her face. She inhaled the oxygen eagerly, drawing in deep breaths, and her panic began to subside.

Meanwhile, Alan busied himself solving the puzzle of the snarled tube on Eloise's dangling mask. With a few deft twists and turns, he freed the mask and handed it back to his sister. A look of self-satisfaction wreathed his chubby face.

Eloise returned Alan's mask and slipped on her own. Almost instantly she tore it off again, yelling, "Alan, you dummy, this thing still isn't working. What did you do to it, you little brat? I still can't breathe! Mom…Dad…help me!"

Calmly, Alan reached up and tugged lightly on the plastic line from which her mask was suspended to initiate the oxygen flow. A look of disbelief crossed Eloise's face as she once more drew in the life-giving element. She turned slowly, slipped her arm around her smaller brother, lifted her mask, and said softly, "Thank you, Alan."

By now, both Inga and Brandon had managed to reach the scene. "Alan, that was a very brave thing to do for your sister," Inga told him, patting his shoulder.

Recompense

*

"Yeah, Alan, you're a real hero." Brandon reached to shake the youth's hand. "Now, we'd better get back to our seats and get our own masks back on or you'll have to rescue *us*, too!"

A look of absolute astonishment spread over Alan's round face, replaced gradually by one of such intense pleasure and pride that he appeared to become one broad, all-encompassing grin. He looked back to be sure his mother and father had heard, then glanced around to see if other passengers were also aware of his heroism. Brandon began a slow, rhythmic clapping, and soon the entire area around them resounded with applause, as well as with muffled shouts of, "'Way to go, Alan!"

The youngster beamed, almost aglow with elation. In the delighted look, Brandon thought he could detect a dawning realization: it really *was* possible to get attention through *positive* actions, rather than only by fussing and whining. Alan basked in his new world of acclamation.

The distraction created by the oxygen masks had given Captain Schisler time to bring Flight 1247 down to a safe altitude, where cabin pressure was finally stabilized. In a relieved voice, still muted by his own mask, he informed the passengers, "Ladies and gentlemen, we have achieved our new cruising altitude of 10,000 feet. All nearby airports have been alerted regarding our predicament and will keep this flight path clear of other aircraft."

An audible sigh of relief emanated from the passengers, despite continuing uncertainties, as the pilot went on, "We are now approximately sixty minutes from Boston International. Although our descent to 10,000 feet means we will consume fuel considerably faster than at FL240, our fuel supply should be sufficient to get us to Boston without any diversions. Thank you all for your courage throughout this entire emergency."

Scattered applause greeted the encouraging news. Most of the passengers appeared to relax, glancing at their neighbors, although an undertone of anxiety remained. When Inga announced that oxygen masks were no longer necessary, passengers happily freed themselves of the devices, and relieved chatter filled the cabin. Attendants moved busily about, assisting and reassuring wherever possible.

"Well, Brandon, it looks like we may have dodged the proverbial bullet," Father Hochburg observed. "That was close, wasn't it?"

"A little *too* close for my comfort zone. This whole episode was a first for me, and I certainly hope it's also a last."

The priest chuckled, "I'm glad none of my parishioners could hear me humming that Protestant hymn while all this was going on."

"What hymn is that?"

"'Nearer My God to Thee.' You mean you didn't hear me?"

It was Brandon's turn to chuckle. "No, Father, but only because we were both humming the same tune."

As she made her rounds checking on passengers, Inga stopped briefly at their row with the observation, "Well, it looks like you two survived in one piece."

"Only on the outside," Father Hochburg informed her. "Inside, we're in shambles."

Inga turned to Brandon. "I hope all of this hasn't made you have second thoughts about the layover in Boston." Her tone was light, but it held a current of concern.

Brandon's broad grin and the intensity in his eyes indicated that she didn't need to worry. "Not a chance! All of the planetary forces combined couldn't make me change my mind. Not now!" He reached out and took her hand gently in his. "Somehow schedules and organized plans don't seem so important when you realize how tenuous life can be."

Inga's eyes sparkled as she squeezed his hand in return. "I couldn't agree more, Brandon. Now, if we can only get this plane safely to Boston, we'll *all* be happy."

"Is there some other problem we don't know about?"

Recompense

⟨∞⟩

"Well, as the Captain told you, when we have to fly at this low altitude it takes a lot more fuel. He thinks we'll have enough, but it's going to be close."

"What happens if we don't?"

"Don't even think about that," she answered with a nervous laugh. Then she continued in a low voice, designed only for Brandon and the priest, "Actually, if the fuel gets too low, as I understand it, the fuel boost pumps fail. And if the engines don't get enough fuel, they just shut down. It's called 'fuel starvation.'"

"That sounds pretty serious!"

"Let's not worry about it for now, okay? Captain Schisler appears confident we can make it. Let's just hope he's right." Inga flashed her most reassuring smile, patted Brandon's shoulder, and moved on.

Brandon looked at Father Hochburg. "Boy, we just never seem to run out of things to keep us on edge on this flight, do we?"

"Maybe it's a test to see how much we can handle before we crack, like with Job in the Old Testament."

"It may not take too much longer to find out, if this keeps up," Brandon replied with a wry smile.

For some minutes, no new emergencies surfaced. The flight held its precarious but steady course, and it appeared that they would soon arrive safely in Boston as anticipated, the hazards of their journey behind them. Brandon leaned back, breathing easier.

An abrupt change in the sound of the jet engines alerted passengers to a new threat. The customary roar had reduced markedly in volume, and the plane's speed slackened noticeably.

Jittery passengers glanced apprehensively at one another, then around the cabin, to see what had triggered this most recent occasion for alarm. Nothing appeared amiss, yet a decided change had taken place.

Expressions of concern were interrupted by the message on the intercom: "Ladies and gentlemen, this is the Captain speaking. As I mentioned earlier, our fuel supply is low, and as a result one of our engines has shut down. I don't want to alarm you unduly, but this does present a serious problem in getting the airplane safely back to Boston."

Captain Schisler was silent for a time, evidently engrossed in dealing with the details of the new emergency. Passengers shifted nervously in their seats, anxious, waiting, uncertain what to expect next. When the Captain came back on, his voice was sober: "I have alerted Boston International of our emergency. Unfortunately, we are no longer within range of any other airports with runways adequate to accommodate an airliner of this size. There is a possibility we may be forced to bring the plane down short of our goal, either in Boston Harbor or the Atlantic Ocean."

Cries of "No! Oh my God, no!" "Not in the water!" greeted this dire announcement, as passengers found themselves once again on the verge of hysteria.

Quickly the pilot continued, in an effort to instill some sense of hope: "Rest assured we will do absolutely everything within our power to get the airplane down safely on land at Boston International. Meanwhile, try to remain calm, and please keep your seat belts securely fastened."

After all they had been through, passengers of Lufthansa Flight 1247 reacted almost stoically to the new crisis. Their nerves frayed, their emotions exhausted by the ongoing crises, they withheld further expressions of despair despite the threat of impeding doom. Instead, travelers appeared to have reached a stage of candid acceptance of their fate, whatever that might be. Many simply sat in quiet resignation, and for the next few minutes an unnatural calm pervaded the cabin, until penetrated once more by the Captain's voice.

"Ladies and gentlemen, we are now beginning preparations for landing at Boston International. Emergency crews there are standing by. At this time we do not anticipate that they will be needed...."

Recompense

∞

Captain Schisler's words were cut short by another dramatic drop in engine noise level, and again the aircraft's acceleration decreased perceptibly. In the relative silence that followed, the former aura of composure evaporated completely, and hysteria threatened to overwhelm the aircraft.

"This is it!" "It's all over!" "We're going down!" echoed everywhere.

Into the bedlam, a tense voice intruded: "Ladies and gentlemen, this is the Second Officer. Another engine has failed, and Captain Schisler and the Co-Pilot are doing everything they can to keep the aircraft on course. Flight Attendants, please begin preparations for an emergency landing. The Captain is doing his utmost to complete the approach with the one remaining engine, so please try to stay calm…and a prayer wouldn't hurt, either!"

With tensions near the breaking point, passengers gripped their armrests or clung tightly to a neighbor or loved one. Through Brandon's mind, a thought kept recurring: Will this be a repeat of Old Oberammergau, with another Kaspar Schisler becoming the instrument of disaster and death? Should he have *avoided* the storm, rather than put all of his passengers' lives in jeopardy, just as the other Kaspar jeopardized the lives of people in historic Oberammergau? Or could we be dealing with some type of "edict" here that dictates history *must* repeat itself?

Through the window, Brandon now glimpsed the pattern of runways that signaled Boston International Airport. He felt a thump as the jet's landing gear came down, then held his breath as Captain Schisler slowly, skillfully guided the wavering plane toward the assigned runway. With a final thrust of the plane, like a last minute grant of mercy, the wheels made contact.

Cheers of relief and gratitude erupted throughout the cabin as realization dawned: the plane was safely on the ground at last! As the jet taxied slowly to a halt at their gate, wild applause continued to reverberate, along with shouts of, "Thank you, Captain, thank you!"

The mood remained euphoric as passengers disembarked. Backslapping and hugging by complete strangers reflected the joy of a group that had been uncertain until now what their futures held in store~or whether they even *had* futures to consider. No one seemed in a hurry. They were happy merely to have survived.

Exuberant expressions of appreciation for Captain Schisler and his crew carried forward as the passengers of Flight 1247 filed from the plane. Brandon straggled behind, exchanging pleasantries and saying his final good-byes to Louise Scheer and Margaret Wilson.

When the Grossfeldts approached, Brandon added a last word of praise for Alan, as he shook the youngster's hand and patted him on the back: "Alan, I'd like to congratulate you again for being such a big help to your sister."

"Ah, it wasn't so much. That's what brothers are for." But the proud smile on the boy's face belied his attempt at modesty.

Parting with Herman and Father Hochburg was particularly difficult for Brandon, but these farewells, too, were finally completed. Now all that remained was finalizing plans with Inga as to where and when the two would meet for dinner that evening. With urgency but without haste, this too was accomplished, and their lingering leave-taking emphasized the pleasant mood of expectant anticipation.

As Brandon finally approached the exit, Captain Schisler extended his hand, looking intently into the young attorney's eyes. "Well, Brandon," the pilot asked earnestly, "what do you think? Has the debt been paid? Has *recompense* finally been made?"

Brandon gripped the proffered hand firmly. "I think the jury just came in, Captain Schisler, and their decision was unanimous. I'm happy to tell you that you have been found 'Not guilty'! Now you're free to go home!"

End

ABOUT THE AUTHOR

Dr. Arnie Zimbelman was a career college history instructor, including teaching a semester abroad in London. Additionally, he and his wife Iris traveled extensively in Western Europe. Attendance at a performance of the Passion Play in Oberammergau, Germany, along with the author's lifetime fascination with "human" history, provided the inspiration for this novel.